Binkie's morning adventure

Binkie of IIIb

Evelyn Smith

Illustrated by H. Coller

Books to Treasure

Books to Treasure
5 Woodview Terrace,
Nailsea, Bristol, BS48 1AT
UK

www.bookstotreasure.co.uk
www.facebook.com/BooksToTreasure

First published by Blackie & Son 1922
This edition 2017

Design and layout © Books to Treasure

ISBN 978-1-909423-87-9

CONTENTS

ILLUSTRATIONS

PREFACE

Constance Evelyn Smith was born in Leamington Spa on 27 December 1885, the eldest of three daughters to Henry Barlett Smith and his wife Eleanor. She attended Leamington High School, where she rose to become head of school, and gained her first-class degree in English from Royal Holloway College. In 1909 Evelyn went to teach English at Glasgow High School but ill health forced her resignation in 1923. She died on 23 March 1928.

BINKIE OF IIIB

CHAPTER I

A SHOCK FOR ROSE

"*Where* did you say they had put you, Binkie?"

Rose Seymour stopped unplaiting the thick rope of hair that hung nearly to her waist, and stared at her small sister with an expression of incredulous dismay. Binkie, clad rather lightly in a shortish striped bath-gown and red slippers that were practically only toes, was tugging the strap of her box with an energy that blinded and deafened her to all that might be going on around her. She took no notice of Rose's question, which was repeated with the sharpness of anxiety.

"Where? IIIB. Why? Isn't that the name? Someone with a tight mouth gave me a little card." Binkie slapped the portion of her bath-gown where a pocket might be. "Oh, of course, it's in my skirt. Hanging up—the side of the wardrobe you said I might have."

Rose crossed the room, found the skirt, and drew out a crumpled card.

"Elizabeth Seymour—Senior School—Form IIIB," she read in slow sad tones, and turned the card over to see if there might be a contradictory statement on the back of it.

"Why—what's the matter?" Binkie sat down abruptly on the floor, as the strap, with the extreme suddenness of its kind, yielded to her efforts. She made neither comment nor complaint, but wriggled round to gaze open-mouthed at the beautiful Rose, standing there in her violet kimono, and looking as if her every belief in human nature had been shattered.

"Are you sorry? What's the matter with IIIB?"

"*Sorry?* My dear child, IIIB is the completest set of duds that has ever been collected in one place since schools were invented. That's what's the matter with IIIB."

"Oh!" said Binkie. She sat back on her heels, still staring thoughtfully at her grown-up Sixth Form sister, who, the infatuated said, was like a princess out of a fairy tale. Binkie wasn't in the least like a princess. Rigged out in a tunic, with a shield and spear, she might have been the smallest soldier in the princess's body-guard: that would have been her fairy-tale place. There was something of the fighter in her whole appearance, in the build of her strong lithe little figure, the set of her head with its bobbed hair, the look of her grey eyes and determined chin. People who did not know them laughed when they saw the two together, because they were so different. People who knew them knew that sometimes, when Rose's eyes grew resolute, and Binkie's grew tender, they were not so different after all. At this moment, as the elder girl contemplated the card with what Binkie called her "sword face", they were rather alike.

"I don't understand it," said Rose. "It's an insult to the family."

Binkie began to look anxious. "The family" meant Rose: Rose, who had had a long triumphant ten years at St. Helen's, climbing from "A" form to "A" form, always in the first place, until, in the Sixth, she became head girl. Binkie had loved to hear her stories, and hold her prizes, and examine her photographs when she came home for the holidays, to triumph there as she did at school. Nothing could be more delightful than to go back with Rose, to travel with her from Waterloo to Reading, and change there for St. Helen's, to see her friends—some of whom had stayed with the Seymours—in the place where she had found them, to make friends of one's own, to do all the funny little things which sounded so amusing when they were described. But Mrs. Seymour had been quite definite on the subject. "I can't do without you both. When Rose goes to college she can come home for week-ends, and then Binkie can go to school at St. Helen's." But suddenly, this Christmas, she had made a new plan. "I don't like to think of Binkie all alone in a new school," she had said. "She shall have a term with Rose there—it will be good for both of them. It may be the only time they'll ever spend together, and they're nice together."

Mr. Seymour had laughed at the notion of Binkie's needing protection. "If Rose could fight her way alone," he said, "surely *Binkie*—"

"Rose never had to fight," said Mrs. Seymour. "She never will. But Binkie may. It's her kind that wants a little looking after."

Mr. Seymour thought that his wife (who was like Binkie) probably knew best, and so it happened that Rose, on her return to St. Helen's, was accompanied by a small, lively, short-skirted figure which jumped and hopped, with a delight such as it had never before known in twelve quite delightful years, at the prospect of starting school at St. Helen's a term before the appointed time.

That delight had not ebbed till this moment. It had all been fun—the journey, the change at Reading, and the quick meal of tea and cake, which Rose ordered with such lordly efficiency; the friendly "Hullo, Binks!" from Lesley Crawford and Rhoda Tyndale, who had stayed with the Seymours in London; the "sisters' room" she was to share with Rose for a term; the school supper and the quick interviews, first with Miss Edmund, the headmistress, then with an unknown, who had given her the little card which seemed to bear such bad tidings. "An insult to the family." Rose, the triumphant certain Rose, was piqued and worried, and Binkie did not like that. She felt that somehow she was responsible, and that it was rather too bad.

"P'r'aps there wasn't room in IIIA," she said uncertainly. "People generally come in September, don't they?"

"M—m—m. They ought to have *made* room in IIIA. What's

the use of having a sister in school if you aren't to have *some* small consideration shown you?"

"I'm not so clever as you," Binkie reminded her. "Perhaps I'm not good enough for IIIA."

"You're *quite* good enough for IIIA," said Rose, refusing to waste time and words in contradicting the first statement. "I think I shall speak to Edmund Ironsides about it to-morrow."

"Oh—had you better? Don't you remember how snubbing she was about the talking in the cloak-room privilege?" cried Binkie, really anxious.

"I told you about that—did I?" Rose was evidently struck with a new possibility of trouble. "Well, remember this carefully, Binkie. You must never, *never*, NEVER repeat anything I may have said to you before I knew you were coming to school. Especially to those beyond-the-limit over-the-edge bounders in IIIB. If you do, you're simply asking for trouble, both for yourself and for me—and you'll get it."

"I won't, Rose. I really won't." Binkie's voice trembled with eagerness to reassure her sister. "I'll be as secret as—as the Hound of the Baskervilles."

Binkie knew nothing of this Hound, but she always alluded to him when she was promising not to tell a secret.

"I don't know about that Hound," said Rose. "But you're a good kid, and I expect it will be all right."

"You won't ask Edmund Ironsides about IIIA, will you?" faltered Binkie, half hoping that Rose would, half fearing least she should involve herself in trouble.

"I don't know. I'm really annoyed about it."

Rose's tone was calmer. She had loosened her hair and was brushing it before the glass. The appearance of the gold-tinged veil of it lying against the new violet kimono was pleasant enough to solace a young woman of seventeen, even if she were not particularly vain about her personal appearance. Her sister sat still by the unopened box looking at her. Suddenly, as if she felt

Binkie's eyes, Rose wheeled round. She was struck by something rather pathetic in the collapse of the excited energy which had flared up in the small figure in the striped dressing-gown, and was annoyed with herself for having, as she put it, "shown Binkie".

"Cut off and have a hot bath, Binks," she said. "And remember to turn on the cold-water tap too, or you'll be boiled alive. I'll unpack your trunk. And don't bother about IIIB. I got rather riled with them because they cheeked me. They may be all right, really."

"Cheeked *you*?"

"Yes. Some people do, you know." Rose laughed, swinging back her long hair. Rose was the sort of person who could laugh at things like that, but Binkie felt a little dismayed. If IIIB cheeked a grown-up sister, who was really rather wonderful, and whom most people adored, what might they not do to her? But, if Rose didn't care, she wouldn't care either.

"You may have some of my bath salts, if you like," said Rose. "Just for to-night, mind. And you had better forget all I said about IIIB. Considering what I am capable of being, I am rather an ass sometimes."

"You're a darling!" Binkie, who loved baths that smelt of violets, seized the big fragrant tin and hurried off, all of a sudden pleased and excited again, and quite indifferent to what next day and the whole term might have in store for her as a IIIB girl.

CHAPTER II

BINKIE'S FIRST DAY

Whatever the circumstances, to be a new girl is not an amusing experience, but it is more easily to be endured if you are one of a small herd, arriving with it and driven kindly if impersonally about by some responsible mistress until you have acquired a little simple essential knowledge about the duties, manners, and customs of school. Binkie was not particularly shy or sensitive, but, when Rose left her at the top of a short corridor inscribed Forms III, she rather wished that someone had been with her, someone before whom she would have been obliged to keep up an indifference, which, after having been feigned for five minutes, would have become real. Rose had said: "I don't think I'll take you and show you to Miss Loraine. It looks so fussy. Just drift in at that door and give her your card and await developments." Binkie had agreed enthusiastically. It was only after Rose had disappeared that she realized she was very new, and that she would have been prepared to chance the imputation of fuss. Better not to consider, but plunge. Quickly she turned the first handle and walked as boldly as she could into the middle of the room, towards a desk where a very capable-looking mistress with a hawk face was sorting papers. As this lady seemed far too busy to be interrupted, she stood still by her side, holding out the card so that, when the alert eyes glanced up, they should at once meet the information that here was Elizabeth Seymour of IIIB.

It was a pleasant room, with neatly arranged desks, glasses of blue and white hyacinths, and a bowl of violets. Evidently it had a little library of its own, for one girl was standing by a shelf of brightly-bound books, entering dates of return or renewal.

Another was pinning up on a big sheet of grey paper pictures of the happenings of the week from an illustrated paper; another was watering the flowers from a little green can. Two or three talked hockey; two or three Latin exercise. Now and then an extra loud burst of laughter occasioned a warning push and "S—s—s—sh!" and a quick glance at the hawk lady, who never looked up. Evidently she was on the best of terms with her class. Binkie thought they looked nice. She wondered uneasily why they were "duds", and which had cheeked Rose.

"*Oh!*" said the hawk lady, suddenly swooping round upon Binkie. "And who are you?"

Just for a moment Binkie really didn't know. Mutely she stretched out the card, thankful she had it to solve the problem so easily.

"IIIB?" said the hawk lady. "But *this* is IIIA."

Binkie's spirits sank lower. The tone, allowing for grown-up modification, was so like Rose's for IIIB. It seemed to her that the whole form of strange girls paused in its various occupations and looked at her, a little contemptuously, a little pityingly.

"Myra! Take Elizabeth Seymour to Miss Loraine, to IIIB."

A tall and spruce girl came at once from a group by the window. Her hair was very fair, her blouse very white, her tie very blue. Binkie liked her beautiful freshness: she was like an advertisement for "Lux" or "Omo". She did not look at Binkie. She led the way down the short passage, opened a door, and stood aside to let the new girl pass in, saying: "*That* is IIIB." There was no sympathy in her voice or bearing; she was as completely detached as if Binkie had been a chair or a pile of exercises, and she disappeared so quickly from the door of IIIB that it seemed impossible for her to have been there a second ago.

"Well, I'm right this time, anyway," Binkie told herself, attempting reassurance, for she knew that she was nearly feeling snubbed. "It's so nice to be right." And she stood looking with the new girl's look round the room in which she now found herself, rather uncomfortably conscious that being "right" was the only nice thing she could possible experience at the present moment.

It was a large room, and might have been attractive, for there were two big windows. But the walls were shiny greenish-yellow, and on them hung askew the pictures that sometimes get into schoolrooms: a large engraving of the Prince Consort on horseback, a faded view of a ravine, and a blurred group of schoolgirls of, say, 1892, in blouses with big puffed sleeves and funny little sailor hats. On one window-sill was a dusty aspidistra and a hyacinth-glass containing a branch of catkins, which looked as if it dated from last year; the other was heaped with cases, books, jumpers, gym. tunics—anything IIIB liked to put there. The desks were out of line; the blackboard uncleaned. Groups of girls whose looks Binkie didn't much care for lolled about. Some of them talked and laughed noisily, with quick self-conscious glances round, as if they were trying hard to be funny; others sat staring in front of them, half asleep. At the mistress's desk was a small absent-minded looking figure, evidently unhappy in her surroundings and doing her best to forget them.

"Oh—*another!*" she said, as Binkie held out the card.

It wasn't encouraging. Binkie stood in mute apology for her existence, while the nearest group of girls stopped talking and stared at her. One of them had a large sweet in her cheek, and the bulge of it made her face look curiously insulting as she eyed the new girl, who, heartened by a sudden vivid dislike, steadily eyed her back.

"Seymour—" said Miss Loraine. "Oh—Rose Seymour's sister, are you?"

There was a faint glimmer of hope or interest in her voice, and Binkie at once responded to it.

"Yes," she said. "Father thought I shouldn't come to school till September, but Mother said I should come this term to be with Rose for a little bit. I shan't get the chance of being with her ever again, probably, you see."

She looked eagerly at Miss Loraine to discover if, by advertising herself as a connection of the head girl's, she had made herself more welcome—she badly wanted to be welcome. Miss Loraine looked nothing but tired; IIIB, however, had changed its expression to one of contempt. IIIA would have done the same, for new girls should not chatter; but IIIA would have been intolerant of gossip about what Father and Mother had said; IIIB was intolerant of the claim to kinship with Rose. Binkie at once saw that she had made a mistake, and got rather red.

"Oh—yes," said Miss Loraine, as if she were trying to collect her wits to consider the question of Elizabeth Seymour, relation to Rose, and what was to be done with her or said to her. "Well, you'll want a book-list and things, I suppose, and a desk to sit at."

She looked moodily about.

"I don't really mind," said Binkie, anxious to put everything right. "I'll use Rose's old books, anyway—and I can easily sit on that stool over in the corner.

Miss Loraine, with startling suddenness, displayed energy. "Oh, impossible," she said. "Quite impossible. Ethel—Sue—Lilian—Grace—move up and let me see if there is a desk in the back row."

There *was* a desk in the back row—one of those ownerless desks into which it is so convenient to shoot surplus property. A low, ominous, grumbling sound rose from the four girls addressed, as they unwillingly and noisily dragged themselves a little to the left.

"*There* you are!" said Miss Loraine, with an expression of weary triumph. Binkie, feeling as if an extraordinary concession had been granted her, began cautiously to make her way across the many obstacles that choked the passages between rows of desks to the place which was to be hers. Instantly the four girls flowed from the left and closed up over the empty seat. The others laughed, and Binkie, feeling it was the only thing to be done, smiled, while her heart felt tight with mortification.

"*Girls!*" said Miss Loraine, obviously trying hard to care. "*Girls!* Move back at once and let Elizabeth Seymour come in."

"But," objected a thin individual, whom Binkie would have liked if she had not been too much embarrassed to like anyone, "I simply can't spare that desk, Miss Loraine. It's my waste-paper basket."

"There *is* a form waste-paper basket, Susan," said Miss Loraine, and looked furtively behind the easel which bore the blackboard, as if she felt that there might not be one, after all.

"It's always so full," objected Susan. "It would look so horribly untidy with my things in it too."

"You shouldn't have untidy things," stated Miss Loraine absently.

"I know," said Susan. "That's what I want to prevent. There's all my rubbish in that desk, as snug and safe as can be."

"Don't be silly, Susan," snapped Miss Loraine, with another sudden spurt of energy, which didn't seem to belong to her, but to be imposed upon her by some mysterious external force. "Clear out that desk *at once.*"

Susan began to clear it with speed. Binkie watched her, wondering how anyone who looked so clean could have such grubby possessions. She was as fresh as the Omo and Lux individual who had shown the way to IIIB; her little, fair, bobbed head shone with brushing; her white blouse was laundered with an efficiency which would have appealed to Rose, who was particular about her linen; the clean-cut lines of her features and figure made the other girls in the back row look frizzy and heavy. Binkie wondered if it was she who had "cheeked" Rose. She knew it might quite well have been, and she was rather sorry to know.

"There it is," said Susan. "It's dusty. But new girls always have pen-wipers. A nice soft pen-wiper would be just the thing to finish off that desk and make it look a perfect treat."

Binkie wasn't sure to whom Susan addressed this theory. Miss Loraine had drifted sadly away, and was looking at the catkins as if she saw them for the first time, which was quite likely; the rest of the back row talked to one another. Perhaps she ought to attempt an answer.

"I haven't a pen-wiper," she said timidly.

Susan looked at her critically and pityingly.

"I'm sorry about that," she said. "But you could always borrow your sister's powder-puff."

Binkie flared.

"Rose hasn't a powder-puff," she said curtly.

Susan looked at her again.

"Hasn't a powder-puff?" she repeated. "No pen-wiper—no powder-puff. Well—well—well—!"

She shook her head as if reluctantly obliged to give up the family as a bad job, and jammed down her desk-lid in a useless attempt to make it close upon the welter within, while whiskers of string and paper protruded from both sides, and the hinges creaked threateningly. Binkie, as unostentatiously as possible, slipped to her place, and, drawing out the books Rose had given her last night, saying they were probably the ones she would need, softly put them in the desk, hoping to attract no further attention, but uncomfortably conscious that Susan's grey eyes were fixed upon her, and that conversation would shortly be resumed. She was not wrong.

"I say," said Susan, in a surprisingly gentle voice, "are you *really* Elizabeth Seymour?"

"Yes."

"And what do they call you? Bessie—Betty—Eliza—Lizzie—what is it?"

"Binkie."

"Binkie? I knew a canary called Binkie once. And Rose Seymour is really your sister?"

"Yes."

"It's a chance," summed up Susan reflectively. "The chance of a lifetime."

With discomfort that increased every moment Binkie
wondered why. She badly wanted to hurt Susan—to give her a
good sharp smack or to push her hard, but she was not used
to smacking or pushing people, and it is not so easy to begin.
So she sat still, clenching her small hands under her desk. She
realized that the other girls were looking at her: some openly,
some furtively. She heard whispers of "Rose—Rose Seymour—
her sister—swank—Binkie?—Binkie Seymour?" Had she not
been a fighter, she might have cried. As it was at least two tears
wanted quite badly to come out, but she held her head so high
that it was impossible for them to do it.

A bell rang.

"Oh—prayers!" said Miss Loraine, as if struck by a happy
thought.

The girls shuffled into line, Binkie at the end, and marched
down to the big hall, where, in neat lines, the school stood for
morning prayers. Or rather, they trailed—IIIA marched.

Binkie could not see Rose: she could see only the tail-ends
of the forms, and Rose stood at the top of the Sixth. But, when
prayers were over and notices had been given out, and someone
began to play a march, Rose led the Sixth Form line from the
hall. Binkie watched her coming down towards the door, with
her fair head held high, and her light triumphant walk. At first
she looked straight in front of her, but, as she passed the tail-
ends, she looked sideways to find Binkie, and gave her a little
smile.

Instantly IIIA turned round as far as it dared, for its hawk
mistress had her eye on it, and looked at Binkie.

Binkie realized that every one of them had been watching
Rose come down the hall, and that every one wanted to know to
whom she had smiled.

Her heart lifted. She didn't care a rap for IIIB, and she was
tremendously proud of Rose.

CHAPTER III

GETTING TO KNOW IIIB

One of Binkie's boy cousins, the same age as her elder sister, had once described her as "such a matey little fellow". He was quite right. She had not often been snubbed, for the people she had known at home had liked her, and she had nearly always liked them. In spite of what Rose had said, and her own first impressions, she was prepared, half-way through the morning, to be interested in IIIB. Miss Edmund, the headmistress, taught them Scripture for an hour after prayers, and, in a miraculous way, the whole form tidied itself up for her. Susan's waste-paper was no longer to be seen. Miss Loraine herself vaguely cleaned the board, and, after searching for a little in a press which seemed awkwardly full, found a piece of chalk, which was laid out ready for use. No one watered the aspidistra or threw away the catkins; but Miss Edmund was short-sighted, and probably thought the window-sill was adorned with fresh and charming decoration placed there by ardent young lovers of Nature. She always knew, however, when personal property was strewn about the room—all headmistresses know this by instinct—and Binkie stared open-mouthed at the masterly way in which the form, assisted by a rather worried Miss Loraine, cleared impedimenta from shelves and stuffed them under desks. She was amazed, too, by the demeanour of the form in the presence of Edmund Ironsides. To be sure, from what Rose had said, she knew this lady to be awe-inspiring—but then so was Rose, though perhaps in rather a different way, and IIIB had no respect for Rose. But they had for Miss Edmund. She evidently found them trying; but Binkie wondered whimsically what she would have thought of them if she had known what they could be. They were now anxious to please—she should have seen them when they were anxious to displease. "She doesn't know when she's well off," said Binkie to herself, watching Susan, with her hands folded and an expression of strained attention on her face, and the unsmiling countenances of her fat and frizzy neighbours. A lot of the girls were rather fat and frizzy, with what Rose called picture-house faces. They seemed too old for the form; others seemed too young; others looked delicate, and were evidently doing all they could to spare their health in school. The odd thing was that none of them seemed to understand what Miss Edmund said, and, though she was cross, she was interesting. One profoundly satisfied-looking individual in large round glasses made a point of carefully raising her hand in answer to every question—but she always answered a question that hadn't been asked. This had such an effect on Miss Edmund that Binkie trembled for the girl's safety—though, mercifully, she did not seem to realize her own danger.

"Who's that?" Binkie could not resist asking, directly the lesson was over, though Susan's demeanour did not invite questions.

"Ah-h-h-h!" said Susan. "That's what I am constantly wondering myself."

Binkie turned a little red, feeling mortified. According to all home standards, Susan was horribly rude, and yet, somehow, she wasn't.

"That's Mona Manders," said a voice from the other side. "She's awfully clever, and will probably be moved into IVA next term."

Binkie looked a little enviously at the satisfied spectacles. She was surprised to know that Mona Manders was clever.

"I wonder if I shall be in IVA next year," she said.

"My word! I wonder!" said Susan.

Then Miss Wingfield came in to teach English. Binkie had never had a Shakespeare lesson before, and she thought it an exciting experience. She liked the mistress's brushed-back fair

Binkie began reading the letter from Macbeth

Jackie began reading the letter from Macbeth ...

hair, and she liked the way the corners of her mouth twitched while IIIB was saying its poetry. Anyone else might have been cross or desperate. Binkie wondered why they said poetry like that, and when they began to read, she wanted to laugh. She thought at first that they must be doing it on purpose, to tease Miss Wingfield, but it was so uniformly bad, and they were so serious about it, that she felt it must be accidental. Reading was so exciting—to stand up, holding a book, and be someone quite different from Elizabeth Seymour must be a glorious sensation. She ached and fidgeted with impatience as they fumbled through the opening scenes of *Macbeth*, and nearly fell off her seat in her eagerness to answer the questions the mistress asked about people and meanings. But, although she had done so much to attract attention, it was with pure astonishment that she heard Miss Wingfield say, at the opening of Scene V: "New girl—what's your name? Elizabeth Seymour?—read Lady Macbeth."

Not having a book of her own, she seized her neighbour's, sprang up, and—quite oblivious to the aggrieved glances of Susan, who seemed deprived of all that was nearest and dearest to her—began to read the letter from Macbeth. It was glorious to have such a chance! The dreadful prayer, which spread a little web of cold across her cheek, was better still; and, when Miss Wingfield said: "Oh, sit down, Mona. I'm going to read Macbeth myself", it was best of all. The lesson left Binkie with beating heart and shining eyes, all doubts as to her luck in being in IIIB gone. But they were soon to return. Directly the fair-haired mistress had gone from the room the form turned upon her.

"I suppose you call yourself an actress," suggested the girl who had supplied information about Mona Manders.

Susan looked sadly at her, shaking her head slowly, and feeling it with her hands.

"It's in the family," she said. "It's in the family."

"*What's* in the family?" said Binkie curtly. She was still elated, and had courage.

"Swank," said Susan.

"There's your *Macbeth*," said Binkie, banging it down rather sharply on the desk.

"Say thank you," said Susan. "Thank you, nice, kind Susan, for lending Rose Seymour's sister, swank minor, your *Macbeth*."

"Thanks," said Binkie curtly.

Suddenly she was perfectly certain it *was* Susan who had "cheeked" Rose.

CHAPTER IV

GETTING TO KNOW IIIA

Binkie did not tell Rose much about IIIB, and Rose was too wise in the ways of school to ask her. Although neither confidence nor sympathy was given, the little girl found comfort in the mere "being with" the big one. Rose, not generally talkative unless she were amused or excited, told her about the idiosyncrasies of the mistresses, what you were likely to get for supper on the different days of the week, and the hedge in the garden where the birds nested. Also she offered her bath salts. Binkie's sense of justice and politeness made her protest: "Oh no, Rose," but Rose said she really meant it, and put a handful into Binkie's sponge-bag, which, by some odd chance, had no hole in it. She was like that every night, and Binkie, always a little sore and annoyed after a day with IIIB, was grateful, although she knew that the unfriendliness of the class was in some mysterious way due to her sister.

She tried to make the best of it, but it was not easy, and soon she began to grow distrustful of herself, and afraid that all forms would regard her with hostility like that of her own. She was quite frightened when, one morning about a week after the beginning of term, Miss Loraine told her that Miss Page, the music mistress, wanted to give her a trial lesson during the IIIB gym. period, and so she must take gym. with IIIA that afternoon.

"Oh, must I really?" she cried, with such obvious dismay that Miss Loraine was moved to reassure her.

"It's only for this week, you know," she said. "It'll be a good chance of getting to know some of the girls in IIIA, won't it?"

"Oh yes!" breathed Binkie, wondering if any mistress at

St. Helen's had a notion of what getting to know girls was like.
All through the morning she hoped that Fate would perform
some kindly conjuring trick which would make it impossible
for her to take gym. with IIIA in the afternoon, and, when, in
her cool short-sleeved white blouse and blue tunic, she found
herself forming into line with these unknown and therefore
doubly dreaded ones, her heart thumped so hard that she felt
the gym. mistress would notice and tell her to stop it until the
class was commanded to stand at ease. Then an astonishing
thing happened. Far from being critical and objectionable, IIIA
were friendly and nice. There was no chance of prolonged
conversation, but in a dozen ways they showed that they were
glad she was there, and wanted to like her, and make her enjoy
the class. Her partner, the girl who had shown her the way to IIIB,
and who, she discovered, was called Myra, smiled at her, and they
did the exercises they had to do together well. One Cecil Drake,
Myra's friend, said "Oh, *good!*" when she swung from one rope to
another; which was handsome of her, as this was a performance
which she herself did particularly well. Two or three girls ran
forward to ask her to dance when the gym. mistress told them to
take partners for the morris. Binkie had forgotten that she could
be so happy, and stored up the pleasure of their friendliness to
tell Rose that evening. Rose would be glad to hear that she had
drilled with IIIA, and that they had been so kind to her.

When the class was over, IIIA proceeded from the gym. into
the little cloak-room that jutted out at the head of the steps leading
into the garden, to change their tunics and make themselves
smooth and clean for half an hour of prep. before tea. They had
worked so hard that Binkie had thought they must be tired, but, as
soon as the gym. mistress had left them, they were possessed by
a fury of energy. Some of them sang and whistled; some, out of
sheer high spirits, jumped on and off the high windowsill of the
cloak-room; one tiny girl thrust her "bobbed" head into a basin
of water, and ran shaking it as if she were a wet puppy trying to

dry his coat. And Cecil Drake turned six quick somersaults along a wooden bench, and boasted that she could say any speech of Henry V's while doing so. Challenged by her friends, she repeated the performance, while emitting a strange guttural sound.

"You *weren't* saying one," said IIIA indignantly. "You *can't* say it."

"Well, I was thinking it anyway," she retorted, with some indignation. "I'll do it again, if you like. Just listen hard, all of you." No one did listen, but, undaunted, she began her somersaults once more, amid a din of applause and laughter. Binkie thought she had never heard so much noise in so small a space. Then, all of a sudden, the door was thrust open. Instantly there was silence—silence such as that which prevailed when Miss Edmund came into a room. Cecil tumbled off the bench and began to comb her hair as if its neatness were her sole object in life. Every one in IIIA assumed that peculiar air of unblemished virtue worn by a schoolgirl who has just broken a rule, or a spaniel who has stolen the chops. Binkie, who happened to be behind the door, thought the position well worth the quite painful push she had received when it was opened. Then the person who had worked this miracle of peace and order spoke, and Binkie stood transfixed with surprise and embarrassment. For it wasn't Miss Edmund. It wasn't even Miss Squire. It was Rose.

"Do you know that you are supposed to be quiet in this cloak-room?" a biting silver voice was saying. "Do you? Perhaps you don't?"

IIIA said not a word.

"Aren't you the people who got a conduct shield last year, IIIA?"

IIIA thought there was no harm in agreeing to this.

"I thought I had heard something of the kind. Will you please be as quick as you can? I suppose I must wait here until you are all out."

Rose's voice was distant, weary, and bored. She was not angry, but unmeasurably scornful. Binkie prickled with dismay. IIIA had been so friendly—now they would be angry and irritated and hold her responsible for Rose's treatment of them. She waited in her safe place until all the others had gone quietly out, and Rose had passed down the steps into the garden, then she crept nervously into the open.

Alas! There stood Myra and Cecil. She could hope for no mercy at their hands. For a minute she contemplated running away in shameless panic, then, setting her teeth, she stood still and waited for them to come up to her, which they at once did.

"Hullo!" said Myra. "Do you like IIIB?"

" Hullo!" said Cecil. "Wasn't that bad luck?"

"It might have been Miss Edmund," said Binkie, wondering what to say for the best.

"Edmund Ironsides? Might. But wasn't. Never is. Just my luck."

Cecil was looking extraordinarily meek and distressed.

"Cheer up!" said Myra, in a matter-of-fact voice. "She won't bear malice. I don't suppose she even saw *you*. It would be quite easy to overlook you in that crowd. What do you think, Binkie?"

Binkie thought it would have been most difficult, so said nothing.

"Of course she *won't* bear malice," Cecil consoled herself. "Splendid characters like that never do."

Binkie looked at Cecil in alarm. Now it was coming. But she was mistaken.

"Binkie isn't at all like her, is she?" said Myra, examining Binkie with interest.

Cecil looked as if she really would have liked to do something for Binkie.

"No, I'm afraid she isn't," she said at length. "'But, though every feature was out of joint, the girl had a strange beauty of her own.' ... I say, Binkie, tell me one thing—what does Rose like to eat?"

"Pickled cabbage," said Binkie instantly, "and horse-radish and chutney and walnuts and pickles and mint-sauce—anything that makes meat interesting."

The two looked downcast.

"Well," said Myra, "I hope you're sure of your facts. We meant to give her a very extra special box of sweets on her birthday, Cecil and I, as a mark of our appreciation of the way she discharges her duties as head girl. Mind, if we do, you're not to eat *one*. They're for her, and her alone."

"She'll probably make me eat *one*," said Binkie. "But I'll take a little hard one—the littlest in the box."

"That's the right spirit," said Cecil approvingly. "But look here, Myra, we probably should get better value in pickles than in sweet-stuff. Sweets are still dear."

Myra groaned.

"Pickles don't seem right, somehow," she said. "Who ever heard of a beautiful singer being acclaimed with hot-house bouquets and bottles of chutney?"

"But Rose isn't a singer," said Binkie quickly. "She's always a little flat."

"It isn't for you to say so if she is," said Cecil severely. "The principle's the same, isn't it? But I don't see why we shouldn't give the darling pickles, if she likes them. We could tie them up with blue ribbon—I've a superb piece—and stick a red rose from my garden and a white one from yours in it. They would be quite poetical pickles by the time we had finished with them."

"Are you sure she likes them?" said Myra, giving Binkie a little poke, as if to surprise the truth out of her.

"Positive, certain, sure," said Binkie.

Further avowals were prevented by the abrupt appearance of Rose at the bottom of the steps. Myra and Cecil at once hurried through the gym. into school, while Binkie, wondering which was the more amazing, IIIA's admiration or IIIB's hostility, ran down to join her sister.

"Are they nice, those girls?" she said at once. "Do you like them?"

Rose raised an indifferent eyebrow.

"Who—Myra Lancing and Cecil Drake, weren't they? Oh yes! IIIA are a bit excitable, but they're good people, all of them, really."

"I wish I were in IIIA," said Binkie.

"Oh, well, hold on to them if they're inclined to be friendly, and don't mind the other lot," said Rose.

Binkie wrinkled up her forehead, and at the same moment she was aware that someone else was frowning as she walked past. It was Susan, her expression as haughty a one as her impish features could manage. She seemed so oblivious of the existence of Rose and Binkie that she must have known that they were there, and looking at her.

She had heard what Rose had said. Both knew that. Rose thought: "Do her good!" and was rather glad; Binkie wished she hadn't.

CHAPTER V

SUSAN AND ROSE

On the following afternoon Myra and Cecil seized Binkie and walked her down to the form gardens, asking questions about Rose, and incidentally imparting much useful information about school. Binkie had already discovered that no one, even one's own sister and head girl, knew what really mattered in the Third except the Third themselves. The enormous importance of form feuds did not seem to touch the Sixth—nor did the constant discussion of competition chances interest them—individuals played for school championships in tennis and swimming; as a form they were above such things. It seemed to Binkie that everyone else was trying to win something. There were form hockey matches, tennis matches, swimming matches; on show days a prize for the best-decorated classroom; at prize-givings a shield for the form which had scored highest in every possible physical and mental achievement.

"Don't you get rather muddled, sometimes, remembering all the things you must be good at?" said Binkie.

But Myra and Cecil assured her no, that was not the case, and said that you would never trouble to do anything well at all if you hadn't to defeat anyone else at the same time. Binkie, who was used to socialistic arguments at home, was inclined to dispute this, but Myra and Cecil said that she was too young to understand, and that there was the form garden.

Binkie exclaimed with pleasure, for the IIIA garden was a charming one. Smooth turf surrounded a sundial about which was planted a huddle of gaily coloured flowers; the border opposite the low wall was made into a rock garden; carefully tended beds marked the other two boundaries. Her guides at once asked Binkie to observe that the portions for which they were responsible were planted entirely with roses.

"It's a compliment," they said. "We're entirely off everything else. As far as we're concerned, the rose is the flow-ow-er of all the world, as the well-known song hath it."

"And does the best form garden get a prize?" inquired Binkie.

"Rather! *We* got it last year, when we were IIA. IIIB, IIB it was then, ran us rather close."

"Did it really?" Binkie was excited and pleased for IIIA. "Where is its—our garden?"

"There!" Myra dramatically waved her hand towards the garden bordering on IIIA's. The path was overgrown with moss; the grass was long and shaggy. A few of the more obstinate varieties of May flowers struggled to show themselves among a tangle of weeds. A little shallow pool was thickly scummed with bright yellowish-green.

Binkie's face fell.

"But—I thought—you said their garden was some good."

"So it was—last year. It's splendid luck to have that pool, you know. But there was a terrific row about their garden this spring. A whole lot of our bulbs disappeared, and naturally we got rather agitated about it. We were pretty certain IIIB had something to do with it."

"We thought Susan Crashaw had, at any rate. You see, when we planted our bulbs in the autumn, Cecil and I, Susan dug them all up. She sent them to us packed in a biscuit-box and addressed on a tie-on label, and we thought we were getting a topping box of chocolates from home."

Cecil snorted in reminiscent disappointment.

"And when we met her afterwards," went on Myra, "she said: 'Hullo! didn't your bulbs come up even sooner than you thought they would?' Silly ass!"

At the risk of giving offence, Binkie had to laugh a little.

"What did you do?"

"Hauled her down to the garden and stood over her while she planted them again. I must say she did it quite decently, though she laughed all the time."

"But what about your spring flowers? Susan didn't take them."

"Why?"

"Oh, I don't know. She doesn't look mean."

"I suppose she doesn't," said Cecil slowly, "but she's an ass beyond money and beyond price. Well, anyway, our stuff went— we did some detective work, and found that Etta Wilkinson had been coming like a thief in the night rooting up our crocuses, and sticking them into one of the IIIB plots."

"How horrid!" cried Binkie, with real feeling. "But—Etta Wilkinson is a wee bit queer, isn't she?"

"M-m-m. If she's not too queer to be outside a lunatic asylum, she's not too queer to realize that IIIA bulbs belong to IIIA. That was our point of view, and Rose agreed with us."

"Did you tell Rose?"

"Oh yes. Things like that generally go to a prefect, and she decides whether they had better be reported or not. Rose was perfectly furious. She's rather splendid when she's angry; don't you think so?"

"I don't know. I don't think I've ever seen her angry like that, only a wee bit cross or snarly or disappointed."

"Well, she is. She attacked IIIB at once—a lot of them were hanging about their precious garden at the time, and she gathered them together and told them what a low-down crowd they were—no better than people who sneak into one another's allotments to steal potatoes; slackers, a disgrace to St. Helen's, and so on."

Cecil stopped for a minute to gloat over memories of Rose and IIIB.

"And did they just stand and listen?" inquired Binkie.

"Yes—no—well, it was rather unfortunate that Rose hadn't

got hold of the story quite right in the first place. She muddled the bulbs Susan dug up and sent to us in October with the flowering bulbs Etta Wilkinson had annexed in spring, so she went rather particularly for Susan—"

"It was our fault," put in Myra. "Practically everyone in IIIA told her the story at once."

"But didn't she realize in the end?" Binkie, with some alarm, was beginning to guess how things stood between Susan and Rose.

"Yes—but by that time Susan had said a good lot—Susan has an appalling temper, you know. She'd attack even Edmund Ironsides if she accused her of anything she hadn't exactly done. And Rose was perfectly furious—white and cold, and all of a blaze inside—"

"What happened?" broke in Binkie. She wasn't particularly interested in descriptions of Rose's rare attacks of rage, but she did want to know the result of this one.

"Well, Rose said it was a serious thing, horribly low-down and mean, and must be reported to Miss Lorimer—she looks after the garden, you know. So it was—and she decided that IIIB should be cut out of the competition altogether. So there it is. This is the result."

"Don't they ever touch their garden now?"

"They're supposed to. Miss Lorimer is always sending them out to weed it, but they just don't bother—there's nothing you can slack over as well as gardening, if you really give your mind to it."

Binkie looked wistfully at the neglected garden.

"It seems a shame," she said. "I don't know how they can keep a garden like that."

"Oh, that's IIIB all over," said Myra. "Sorry, Binkie—but you aren't a bit like the rest of them, you know. I don't believe any of them ever would have worked at it if it hadn't been for Susan. She was tremendously keen—always getting a tuft of something from uncles in Australia or South Africa or Dumfries or somewhere—you know the kind of thing. And she spent all her Saturday money on seeds, and all summer risked bad dorm. marks for being out killing slugs when the rest of the form was in bed."

"Poor Susan," said Binkie.

"She's a limitless ass, you know," said Myra. "And she was dreadful to Rose."

Binkie opened her mouth, then shut it again very quickly and tight. With a little prick of horror she realized that she had nearly said "Wasn't Rose rather dreadful to her?"

It would have been unforgivable if she had said it—Rose's own sister, who thought her a wonderful person, to Rose's satellites, who seemed to regard her as a kind of goddess.

School was a queer place—it made you do and feel queer things. She must be very careful.

CHAPTER VI

A Plan and a Match

Binkie could not forget that IIIb garden.

All her practical knowledge of flowers was confined to lobelias, geraniums, marguerites, and fuchsias in balcony tubs and window-boxes, and she had always longed for a garden. In a garden things came gradually—little speckles of green, tiny leaves uncurling into different shapes, buds of whose inside colour you could not be certain, lovely firm petals opening into stars and crowns, cups or bells. Her father had told her about it. He called the pots that came from the florist's ready-made flowers. Binkie liked them, and she was not sure what he meant. Now she had a chance of finding out—part of that IIIb garden must be hers, as she was a IIIb girl. She followed Cecil and Myra to the tennis-courts, but left them almost at once fagging balls for a set in which Rose was playing, and ran back to the form gardens.

She was glad to be alone, as she wanted to examine the place thoroughly. She found a little shed between two laurel bushes, and a fairy-tale sensation came over her as she turned the key in the rusty lock and stepped timidly inside. There was a smell of matting and mould, a row of gardening tools, a shelf containing torn packets of seeds, tangles of string, a bottle of weed-killer, and a basket, a wheel-barrow, and a box half full of earth. To her disappointment she could find nothing that would cut grass. She wanted to see shorn turf, as perfect as IIIa's, round that pool. She shut and locked the tool-shed door and prowled round the beds, wondering which were weeds and which flowers. It would be humiliating to spend an hour in pulling up what might be the garden's most cherished possessions. The pool—what was the right way to clean a pool? Could you skim off that green stuff? Could you plant water-lilies? Binkie felt unusually helpless. The IIIB garden would be a topic Rose would not care for; the girls themselves had evidently chosen to neglect it; Susan would say it was another instance of the family swank if she were to consult Miss Lorimer. With a new shyness bred of school, Binkie dreaded the thought of someone—perhaps a whole crowd—coming past and telling her she was doing the thing wrong, laughing at her. Perhaps it would be Susan—Susan who knew all about gardens. If you were sure Susan liked you it wouldn't matter *what* she said—if you knew she didn't, her remarks stuck in like pins. Binkie wasn't going to risk Susan.

How would it be to get up at five next morning and make a few experiments? Early rising was well known to be a virtue, and as a virtue no whit the worse for being kept secret. Rose slept heavily—there was no fear of disturbing her, and, as her sister was often dressed and out of the room before she was awake, she would not be alarmed at the sight of an empty bed. Her mind made up, Binkie went cheerfully back to the tennis-courts. The older girls had finished for the afternoon, and the III's were beginning to play.

Myra and Cecil beckoned to Binkie, and she was glad to sit by them and watch the game. Four of IIIB were playing as if they thought it a fag on a hot afternoon. Susan sat on a lawn-mower staring at them, with a tiny wrinkle between her brows. Her thin little hands clasped the handle of her racket firmly. Binkie had noticed and liked the way she held things hard. Mona Manders, leaning on the mower, kept up a stream of talk, but Susan paid no attention to anything but the tennis. The IIIA game was unformed but interesting. The players tore about the courts to take balls, tried tremendous dashing serves, kept the score at the tops of their voices, and wasted energy as if they had a limitless supply. In their enthusiasm they got into the queerest attitudes and sent some extraordinary balls, but they were far too much in earnest to laugh.

"I think they'll play well some day," said Binkie, with a giggle of joy she couldn't repress, as a would-be smashing serve ricochetted from the net and hit its sender full and hard in the waist-belt. "They do try so hard, don't they?"

"IIIA always tries hard," said Myra complacently. "We're a sporting crowd, I will say that for us."

"We aren't," said Binkie, with a sigh, as the IIIB game stood still while the server collapsed on the ground in a helpless state of laughter, because she had achieved a double fault. "We're the oddest lot I have ever seen."

"Fuff! Don't worry about that," said Myra. "You ought to be in IIIA. Come and play in our set after this, won't you?"

"It's very good of you," said Binkie, gratefully but uncertainly. She knew that Myra and Cecil's tennis was first-rate, and she had practised with Rose in the holidays and was certain of playing a fairly decent game, but she did not like putting IIIB aside. True, it showed no signs of interest in her, the only girl she liked personally seemed violently to object to her; but it was hers, she belonged to it. She was ashamed of having called it odd—she wished she could unsay her description of it to these pretty, clever, satisfied IIIA's, who got all the prizes and did everything well.

Four o'clock struck, and the games' mistress blew a whistle.

"Forms III, second set," she proclaimed, and went back to a little notebook in which she was doing money sums. Miss Gainsborough was always doing these sums—accounts for hockey teas or travelling expenses or ground upkeep, and she never could get them right. Occasionally one of the mathematical Sixth would be appealed to, and would straighten them out for her, but in a few days the complication would be well twisted again. It was rumoured that in gym. Miss Gainsborough occasionally said: "5*s.* 11½*d.* from 10*s.* 2¾*d.*" instead of giving a word of command, but, as Rhoda Tyndale pointed out, her brain did not work as simply as that, and had the story been true, it would have reported her as commanding: "10s. 2¾d. from 5s. 11½d."

Susan and Mona Manders got up, dragged an unwilling victim to the IIIB court, and looked out for a fourth. A dark girl with an athletic body and quiet eyes came across to Myra and Cecil.

"Coming on?" she asked. "Got a fourth?"

"Binkie Seymour may as well play with us," said Cecil. "She's probably good."

"Does it run in the family?" said the dark girl, with a friendly smile.

How nice they were! Would they think it horribly churlish and ungrateful if she didn't play with them? Binkie's heart began to thump uncomfortably, and she felt herself turning red.

"Thanks ever so much," she said in a low voice, "but won't a IIIA girl want to play in your set?"

"Oh, I don't know," said Myra. "Will IIIB want you?"

Binkie glanced at the IIIB group, which was standing quite near, and which obviously couldn't find a fourth.

"I'm not sure," she said. "Probably not. But still—"

Myra and Cecil looked surprised, and indeed Binkie couldn't understand herself. Fortunately another IIIA girl walked up, and inquired if a fourth were needed. The IIIA set moved off to its court, and Binkie, with a sort of headforemost courage, went up to the IIIB's.

"I say, shall I make up your set?" she asked, looking straight at Susan, who, she knew, had heard the offer of the IIIA girls.

"I suppose you must if you want a game," said Susan coolly. "There isn't another court, you see."

Snubs always struck Binkie full and hard, hurting her tremendously. For a minute she felt a rush of pain and tears, as if someone had hit her nose, and made crying a thing uncontrollable, quite apart from other feelings. Then all of a sudden she became very stiff and strong and certain of herself.

"Yes, I do want a game," she said. "I'll play in your set."

The two other IIIB girls stared at her amazedly; Susan accepted the situation without change of expression.

"Toss for partners?" she suggested.

"No," said Binkie. "I'll play you. The other two can toss."

Susan rounded her eyes.

"You seem to know all about our powers," she commented.

"You and I play about the same," said Binkie, unmoved. "It'll be more satisfactory if we play against one another."

She knew Susan wouldn't like that "play about the same", and Susan didn't.

"Come on, then," she said; "Mona and Lilian, toss, will you?"

In a moment Binkie found herself with Lilian Forsyth, a pretty, delicate, soft-looking girl who held a racket as if she didn't care for the feel of wood, facing the shining glasses of Mona Manders, and the light taut figure of a resolute Susan.

"She'll be terrific," thought Binkie. "But I'm going to win—I'm jolly well going to win."

She was right. Susan was terrific—as terrific as a lightly-built girl of thirteen can be. She meant to win too, and returned every ball to the trembling Lilian, who jumped, hit the air, and gasped: "Oh, I say!" Mona Manders, on the other hand, though she played in the worst possible style, scored points. Her high balls came over with unfailing regularity; she wasn't frightened at a serve that looked worse than it was. Binkie's spirits sank—she wanted badly to win, and it seemed very likely that she would be beaten.

"Look here, I'm going to poach," she said to Lilian. "Hope you don't mind. If you stand right off the court and simply stare at the balls you may get some of Mona's. But I'll take all Susan's—everywhere, except when she serves to you. Sorry, but we *must* win."

Lilian stared with mild blue eyes, showing no resentment. As long as someone else did the work she did not care how the game was played. And Binkie worked—with brain as well as muscle.

She discovered a point on the line where Susan's backhand stroke was slow and weak, she gave her that particular stroke until it was a wonder she did not perfect it. She discovered that, although she tried patiently for every ball, Mona didn't care for running up to the net. She resolutely took every one of the nasty returns Susan sent in Lilian's direction. And Lilian began in an extraordinary way to improve. "Serve any old thing," Binkie implored her, "but don't serve a double fault."

"Oh, good, partner!" she would applaud, when Lilian, standing far back as directed, urged one of Mona's skied balls still farther heavenward, whence deliberately returning to earth it dropped safely just over the net. "Good! Topping! My word, this *is* a game. We're going to win." Lilian couldn't help liking it, and brisking up. It was a tradesmanlike set, and Binkie knew it, but she didn't care. She felt that a whole lot depended on Susan's being beaten then and there, and beaten she should be.

And beaten she was. Rather to her astonishment Binkie found that she was "nervy". Once the game hung in the balance she was likely to lose it. And Mona, who was fat and moved heavily, got tired. The set ended at 6 to 4 to Binkie and Lilian, who had lost the first three games rather ignominiously. Binkie looked across at Susan, who did not look at her, but began to loosen the net.

"Wasn't it a splendid game," said Lilian, with enthusiasm she had never before been known to display. "I shall be stiff to-morrow."

"You wouldn't have won if we had been counting points, not games," said Mona, adjusting her spectacles and looking as satisfied as if the set had been hers.

"Oh, you can't say that now," snapped Susan. "We've lost the game, and that's the end of it."

"It's the first game we've ever played," said Binkie, screwing up her racket-press.

"No reason why it shouldn't be the last," said Susan with point.

"It won't be, though," said Binkie.

For a minute their eyes met. Susan turned away at once, but, quick and uncertain though it had been, there was something in her look which astonished Binkie, and made her long to see it over again, so that she might be sure she hadn't made a mistake.

It was as though Susan, though she didn't intend to do it, badly wanted to laugh.

CHAPTER VII

BINKIE'S MORNING ADVENTURE

Binkie knew that if you want to be sure of waking at five in the morning you must bang your head on the pillow five times before you go to sleep. She remembered to do this, pulling the sheet over her head in case Rose should see and think her mad. Sure enough, just as she awoke, she heard the clock of St. Helen's striking five, and for a few minutes she lay congratulating herself on the success with which she could work a charm. Then she softly got up, one eye on a tail of golden hair which was the only visible sign of Rose in Rose's bed, seized her clothes, and tiptoed across the room into the corridor. She had decided that it would be less risky to dress there.

Safe it might be, but it was unpleasant. Why should a corridor be so much lonelier than a road? wondered Binkie, as, standing on the little grey-and-red mat outside her room, she huddled on her things, looking anxiously up and down the long outside strip, with its rows of painted doors which seemed to bend their look upon her like narrow accusing faces. Corridors and roads are both long, both lead somewhere; people pass and repass along them to get to their rooms or their homes. But roads are under the sky, and corridors under ceilings, and there are all sorts of things on roads besides people—you see hares cross them in the country, sometimes weasels, sometimes, if you are lucky, a fox walking low down, and birds live by them, and you see their wings dart across the hedges. Winds go across roads, but you get only irritating draughts in corridors. Binkie's thoughts of the roads and lanes of St. Helen's and of summer holiday places were so pleasant that she was surprised to find herself dressed and ready for her gardening exploits before she had had time to be depressed by the disapproving look of the corridor.

"I'll undress again when I come back at half-past six, and bathe and do my hair," she thought. "Water makes a noise, and hair takes a long time."

Scissors! She must go back into the room and find scissors to cut the grass. They weren't the proper implement to use, she knew, but they would be better than nothing. Rose had a big pair she used when her annual attack of dressmaking seized her. Generally they were in her work-basket, but, to her dismay, Binkie could not find them there. As she softly rummaged for them, the basket creaked, and Rose turned on her pillow. Binkie stood stock-still, wondering how she could make her reason for early rising sound sensible if she were suddenly questioned, but her sister settled down to sleep again, and, resolved to take no further risks, she seized the manicure scissors that lay on the dressing-table, and hurried out of the room and down stairs.

The big garden lay sparkling in the early morning light, and, as Binkie stepped into it, she felt as she did when she was the first to jump into the swimming-bath. She half expected the light to break round her as the water did, as she plunged down the shallow steps, three at a time, and raced along the terrace, down the bank, across a green parterre, down another bank to the form gardens. It was glorious to be up and out while all the others were in bed, and in her enthusiasm she thought she would get up early always, even when she was quite an old woman. Only she must not talk about it, or everyone would do it, and then it would be necessary to get up a little earlier, and everyone would think so too, and then earlier, till at last you would be getting up before you went to bed. "For goodness' sake begin to work," she commanded herself. "The worst of getting up early is that it makes you think too much, and if your brain spins round like this you'll get nothing done at all."

Inspecting the flower-beds, she found dandelions and

groundsel, which she knew weren't proper flowers for a garden, and she resolved to weed for half an hour, cut grass for half an hour, and in the remaining time do odd jobs. Of their nature she was uncertain, but she had lived long enough to know that, where a set piece of work is, there will odd jobs be. This division of labour would make her do more than if she spent all her time on one thing—and she wanted to do a lot and make a real difference in the appearance of the garden before breakfast.

The chickweed came up easily, but the dandelion roots were another matter. The first broke off short in her hand, leaving a stubbly tuft of sticking-up stalks and leaves—which she knew would give her as much trouble as a broken tooth does the dentist. She fetched a little fork from the tool-house and carefully loosened the soil about the next, but the root broke off sharply when she pulled, and she felt it useless to begin to burrow again. The third she managed to get out whole. "But it looks as if I'd been digging a grave," she thought. She wondered if IIIA got all their dandelion roots out. They would probably make the process interesting by having a competition to see who could extract the longest and most perfect specimen. A good notion—why not a Form Shield or Junior Cup for the finest collection of dandelion roots from the school garden? School was supposed to make you do fairly amiably what you didn't much want to do—to be a real good dandelion-rooter would need far more endurance than to swim well or to play tennis, and would be of more use. Could pigs dig up dandelion roots? Stories always talked of pigs as rooting, as they talked about motors honking and carriages bowling. You might train pigs. ... Binkie's reverie was interrupted and she stood still, while a little web of cold spread over one cheek. A long, loathly worm, glistening with slime, crawled from the excavation she had made. She had never seen one like it before, and for a minute she could not believe that it really was there—was certain she had imagined it. But, as it wriggled another coil of itself into the light, she knew it was true, and, hastily forking a scattering of earth upon it, walked steadily away from the hole. She felt curiously insulted—if such repulsive things had to live in the earth they should bury themselves deep down, and have the good sense and taste not to come up and horrify people. Soberly she began to clip the grass with Rose's manicure scissors. But, although she had plenty of courage to tackle a difficult task, she felt this was hopeless. Opened as wide as it could be, the mouth of the scissors seemed a very small one for the great shaggy coarse tussocks, and the effort of forcing them to cut began to hurt her hand. Also she was conscious of being very hot and hungry. She stood straight up and looked ruefully at the heap of earth with the worm in it, the few handfuls of weeds withering in the sun, and the tiny patch of uneven grass. At this rate she would never improve the garden—it had looked better before she touched it.

The pool! Binkie's heart lightened with a last hope, and with a return of energy she crossed to the little circle of scummy water. She plunged her hands in and fished up trails of weed. The water was deliciously cold. Driven by a sudden desire to immerse more of herself in it, she sat down and tore off her shoes and stockings. Tentatively she put in one foot, and discovered that the pool was tiled. How lovely it might look! She put both feet in and stood up straight—for one small instant. She had not realized that the sides of the pool sloped a little, and were slippery with weed— but she was now to know it. She fell right in—for a second even her head was under water. And, once in, she did not find it easy to get out. For a hopeless minute or two she imagined herself left there till IIIA came to weed their garden, and wondered if she could duck under water if Susan happened to come along, and stay there till she had passed by. Then, by a miracle as it seemed, she managed to heave herself out, and stood dripping, besmeared with mud and scum, weed in her hair, and a tadpole caught in one wristband. She freed him gently and flung him, wriggling with ecstasy, back into the pool. She wondered how anyone, even a tadpole, could be so pleased to live there.

She wrung some of the water out of her skirt, and set off towards the house. One thing was certain—she must tell Rose. Fortunately Rose wouldn't comment too strongly on her mental condition till she had helped her to change and dry her hair. She was a satisfactory person, but no one is really satisfactory company when you are feeling as foolish as Binkie was. She wished with all her might that she had been doing something sensible instead of falling into a pond like a baby. She could have cried like a baby, too, without much effort, in fact she found some difficulty in persuading herself not to do it, as she plodded on through the garden, leaving a trail of muddy water and weed behind her, her soaked clothes coldly dragging round her, the new drops sliding from her hair down her back giving her little new sensations of wetness.

Never had she been so glad to see the flight of low steps leading to the school entrance hall. She broke into a sort of limping run as she approached them, mounted them two at a time, and then stood still in horror.

It must be far later than she imagined—quite half-past seven. IIIB and IIIA girls were hurrying across the landing at the top of the first flight of stairs; Lesley Crawford crossed the hall whistling and went into the little room where the rackets and balls were kept. And coming down the stairs straight in front of her was the person whom of all others she would have been most glad to avoid—Susan Crashaw.

She simply threw up her hand. It was no use pretending that she didn't see Susan, or that Susan didn't see her, or that she didn't feel extraordinarily silly and miserable. She leapt on to the doormat, having just enough presence of mind not to drip on to the white-and-red flags of the hall, and stared at Susan with rather the expression of a young thrush who has got to the edge of the nest and sits there petrified, unable to tell what brought him there and what on earth he intends to do next.

Susan stopped too—but only for an instant. Then she tore

down the stairs, seized Binkie, flung open one of the narrow doors by the big hall one, and jammed her into the little housemaid's cupboard-room behind it. Then Binkie heard a key turned in the lock and drawn from it, and the quick patter of Susan's sandalled feet back across the hall.

She was so completely astounded that she felt neither angry nor scared. What did Susan mean to do? Did she hate her so much that she wanted to kill her—to shut her up till she died, like the lady of *The Mistletoe Bough*? If she did, she would not find it easy. She moved her head a little to avoid the whiskers of the long broom against which Susan had pushed her, and immediately her cheek was brushed by the soft tickly head of a feather mop. Dustpans and a mouse-trap were at her feet, and she rather thought she was standing in a cinder-sifter. The only light on her surroundings came through a narrow grating, high up but wide enough to let in plenty of air. At any rate she would not be suffocated.

When did Susan mean to let her out? She must realize that the maids would not open the cupboard until early next morning—surely she wouldn't risk leaving her till then. But perhaps she was mad—just mad with hating her, and didn't care what she did or what happened afterwards as long as she could make her enemy thoroughly uncomfortable and give her a good fright.

If the first desire had been hers, she had certainly succeeded. In spite of the stuffy atmosphere of the cupboard, Binkie was shivering with cold, and she felt faint with hunger. She wondered if she would have enough voice to cry out—and decided she wouldn't—it would really be easier to stand still and endure till deliverance came.

A sound—the sound of a key being fitted softly and cautiously into the lock. Binkie shrank back, her heart beating hard. Then the door opened a little and a hand thrust in a bundle.

"Hustle!" said a low voice. "Put your wet things in the bag. I'll tell you when it's safe to come out."

Again the door closed, and the key was turned.

Binkie seized the mackintosh "bath-bag" and quickly drew out a scanty swimming costume, a gym. tunic, blouse, stockings, suspenders on a belt, rubber shoes, a towel, and a square of chocolate. Quick as thought she began to strip off her wet clothes, while astonishment even greater than that she had felt when pushed into the cupboard overcame her.

For it was Susan's voice which had given the hurried directions, and the hand which had pushed in the bag of garments was Susan's.

CHAPTER VIII

An Afternoon in the Garden

Five minutes later Susan let Binkie out of the cupboard, and examined her with a critical look.

"Nothing unusual will be noticed," she decided. "If anyone points out that your hair is wet you had better state that you simply couldn't contain your impatience to wash it, so got up early to do it."

"No one will. Thanks most awfully," said Binkie.

"An unexpected pleasure. Push in to breakfast," said Susan briefly. She then seized the mackintosh bag and disappeared upstairs, while Binkie, warm and dry, went into the big sunny room to eat porridge and bread and "mixed fruit" jam with a relish not often associated with school meals. It was odd to sit there as usual, of no particular interest to anyone, when she had felt so certain of having thrust upon her the sort of fame she would much rather avoid. No one in the room had an idea that she had been up early trying to improve the IIIB garden, that she had failed dismally, and had come back looking unusual. No one but Susan, who was consuming her breakfast with the cool detached expression Binkie had once thought affected, but which she now felt to be as much a part of her as her shining fair hair and the beautiful cleanness of her white linen blouse.

She could hardly believe that it was Susan who had helped her so opportunely, and as the day went on she began to wonder if she might have been mistaken, if the episodes of the early morning had not been a vivid half-waking dream. For Susan took not the slightest notice of her in school; in fact, she seemed rather more unfriendly than usual. Binkie had half hoped that they would play tennis together that afternoon—they were splendidly matched, and it must be dull playing at pat-ball with Mona Manders, the only other IIIB who could give Susan any sort of game. But, directly after midday dinner, Susan sauntered off alone, playing a funny little tune on a mouth-organ she drew from her blazer pocket. Binkie knew that this was a habit of hers; she had heard her explain to Mona that she had picked it up from the natives of South Africa. But where she had picked up the tune was a mystery—it was like nothing known in the world of music. When questioned about it she would stop for a minute, say with pitying contempt: "Don't you know *that?*" and resume it *prestissimo*. As Binkie heard it dying away in the distance she felt lonely and disappointed. She couldn't understand why she wanted Susan so badly, and why the society of Myra and Cecil, two of the desirable IIIA's, seemed dull in comparison to what hers might be. It was silly and annoying—when Susan obviously didn't care a screw of paper for her, or indeed for anyone else. She went up to her room, folded up Susan's clothes—which she had changed for her own directly after breakfast, took them to her cubicle, and put them on the bed. She had meant to take them when Susan was there, and thank her for her extraordinarily useful behaviour that morning—but if she didn't intend to be friendly now, she wouldn't persuade her to be.

On the way downstairs she encountered Myra and Cecil, risking their lives in an attempt to view Rose as she passed down the lower corridor, which could be done only by hanging three-quarters of themselves over the banisters and then craning their necks till they nearly overbalanced. She entreated them to stop, and they invited her to come with them to the form gardens. It was a special gardening afternoon, they said, the mowing-machine would be out, and if Binkie would like to help them to cut the grass—

"I'd like to cut the IIIB grass," said Binkie. It was difficult for

her to give up things, and the memory of the morning's despair
was already growing faint.

"Oh, of course, you're IIIB," said Myra. "I'm always forgetting
that. You aren't a bit like one."

"It's so queer to think of Rose Seymour's sister in IIIB," said
Cecil.

"But she's there," said Binkie. "I expect it's her sphere. Anyway,
she quite likes it."

Myra and Cecil looked at her with some astonishment, but she
pretended not to notice. She didn't mean to give them another
chance of telling her she ought to be in IIIA, or of running down
IIIB, not at any rate while she and Susan were in it.

"Well, let's see if you quite like chasing that weary old mower
over your bit of virgin forest," said Cecil. "You'll have a chance
to prove your muscle over that job."

Binkie smiled, wondering what Cecil would have said if she
could have seen her hopelessly clipping away with those manicure
scissors.

"Smile on!" said Cecil. "I expect the mower's smiling inside
more than you'll feel inclined to when you have known it for five
minutes."

"Be quiet, Cecil," said Myra. "You're discouraging the child.
Nice child, too, in her way. Go ahead, Binkie, you can keep that
mower as long as ever you like. Cecil and I will go and look at
our roses."

Binkie seized the smart, reliable-looking machine and trundled
it noisily along the gravel, while Myra and Cecil, extraordinarily
lazy for IIIA enthusiasts, ironically watched her.

"That's it all over!" shouted Cecil. "All talk. If it cut grass as
hard as it rattles! I hate its mean ways."

But Binkie—steadily pushing on through the thick tangle,
seeing a little cloud of blades and daisy heads rise before her
and fall into the red-painted tin hood, and smelling the delicious
earthy green smell she had noticed even in London when grass

was cut in May—felt that she rather liked it. And when she saw the trim strip, ever growing wider, that rewarded her labour, and realized that she was making a big difference to the garden, she felt that she liked it very much indeed.

She was so much engrossed in her work that she did not realize that the IIIA girls had inspected their rose trees, done a little weeding, and gone, and she jumped when, as she turned her machine for the last-time strip, a voice at her shoulder said: "Oh—Elizabeth—are you gardening?"

Turning sharply she saw Miss Loraine, standing dangling a large pair of gardening scissors against her bright-blue dress, while she stared moodily at the heap of grass and daisies Binkie had turned out of the hood, as if, like an unsuccessful crystal-gazer, she expected to see things which refused to appear.

"Well, I'm not exactly *gardening*," said Binkie modestly; "because I don't know how to do it. I'm just cutting grass."

"Oh—yes," said Miss Loraine, turning her gaze upon the lawn-mower, which she contemplated as if she had never set eyes upon such a thing before.

It seemed as if there were nothing else to be said. Binkie didn't like to creak off down that last strip, and turn her back on Miss Loraine, and yet she felt the young woman would be rather relieved if she did abruptly go away and put an end to the interview she had, by a mysterious impulse instantly regretted, brought upon herself.

"Are you going to cut flowers, Miss Loraine?" she asked, suddenly inspired by the scissors.

"Flowers?" said Miss Loraine, vaguely glancing about the weedy borders. "No. I rather think I was going to cut grass."

"Grass!" cried Binkie.

"I suppose it was rather insane of me. I know you don't cut grass with scissors, of course. But it looked so appalling, and I didn't know where the mowing-machine was. I never *do* know where machines are, somehow—and it takes such a long time to do everything by hand."

Binkie laughed.

"I was far worse," she cried. "I was so keen on cutting the grass that I tried to do it with manicure scissors—Rose's, too. Only she hasn't seen them yet."

Miss Loraine underwent one of her sudden changes. Binkie thought she had never seen anything so sudden except the spring to life of a sulky picnic fire when someone heaps larch twigs on it.

"Did you?" she said, as if it were really too good to be true. "Did you really, now? Do you love gardens? I do, but I've never worked in one. Father and Mother were so keen on ours that they wouldn't let anyone else touch it. We had three beds of lilies of the valley—you know the lovely kind that grows in gardens, with a greenish look about the flowers when you stack them into a bunch. And the leaves—rain slips into their leaves better than into any other kind; you have to shake it out when you pick them. There's a bed of lilies over there by that American currant bush—that made me think of them."

"I've never seen them, except in shops," said Binkie. "We had fuchsias and geraniums in our window-boxes, and the lilies were over when we went to stay in the country in the summer. But geranium leaves smell so nice. When I was small I used to think they would make lovely capes for fairy ladies—rather dressy capes, all crinkly and scented up, and with them they could wear gold calceolaria bags to keep their money in."

"So they could. And petticoats of London Pride silk—d'you know how you can skin the inside silk off those thick green leaves? Oh, but you won't know London Pride, as you live in London. There's coltsfoot flannel too—poor people wear the great big leaves lined with thin grey, but the little curly leaves are white and thick and soft inside, even their outside has white filmed over it, and the rich 'infants and invalids' have those."

"And Solomon's Seal grapes," said Binkie, with a chuckle. "They used to be hanging under the leaves, in the garden at Haslemere, in July."

"Solomon's Seal used to grow over our lily beds," said Miss Loraine. "Let's see if there's any of it here."

"Half a minute," said Binkie, forgetting deference. "I'll just run this old mower along the last strip first."

"Right. I'll clear away the grass you've cut," said Miss Loraine.

Binkie rattled off with fresh energy, as delighted as she ever had been in her life. The garden would come right after all, and no one knew and no one ever would know what a failure she had made of her exploits before breakfast.

No one except Susan.

Binkie turned her machine at the end of the strip and saw Susan piling cut grass into a wheelbarrow.

She stood quite still and stared. Three minutes ago neither Susan nor wheelbarrow had been within seeing distance, now they looked as if they had been there for a whole afternoon's work. It must be a IIIA girl. No, it was Susan—she could see the shine of her fair head, and the mouth-organ sticking out of her patch pocket. She was working at a tremendous rate. The speed with which she darted from the barrow, lifted an armful of grass, shot back and dumped it in, leapt to the heap again, was in comic contrast with the leisurely drifting movements of Miss Loraine, who gathered up grass as if it were green silk.

Binkie was curiously dismayed. Susan couldn't have seen her—in spite of the surprising event of that morning it was only too certain that she wanted to have nothing to do with her. Binkie felt as if she simply could not stand another of the sharp painful little snubs Susan gave. She wished she could get one in first—but, to the end of her life, she would never learn how to snub a person intentionally.

Soberly she trundled the mowing-machine back to the path. Had she known it, there was an expression on her little fighting face which rather daunted Susan, who began to carry grass with even greater rapidity than before.

"It might be a beautiful garden," said Miss Loraine.

"It was last year," said Susan.

"I know. It isn't really in very bad order. But it wants a lot of things. ... I'll send home for some things," cried Miss Loraine, with another of her sudden blazes of energy.

Susan looked at her eagerly. Binkie remembered that Myra had said that Susan loved gardens.

"I can get things too," she said.

"The roses will come on all right," said Miss Loraine. "They have been neglected, but they are good ones. And there are irises, I see. We must do something with that pool. It's so lucky to have a garden with a pool."

"Do you like black pansies," asked Susan.

"I like everything but chrysanthemums," said Miss Loraine. "Gardeners curl their hair when they take them to shows, and I'm sure they like it. They aren't real flowers."

"I like the smell of them," said Susan. "You know, however lovely we make this garden, we're out of it. We can't get the form shield. IIIA will have that."

"Oh, bother the form shield," said Miss Loraine.

Susan and Binkie stared at her, and Miss Loraine, remembering that she was a form mistress, got vague and troubled again.

"Oh—I don't mean that exactly," she said. "I like shields and things, you know—it must be exciting to have a form that gets them. Only the garden itself will be so lovely—it'll be such fun to work in it. I do so want to work in it, and perhaps I shouldn't be allowed to if there were any chance of being in for a competition."

Susan looked thoughtfully at Miss Loraine. Binkie knew that she was wondering whether she would be counted as a handicap or an advantage in the struggle. But Susan was liking her, obviously. Binkie was glad.

"What'll *you* get from home for the garden?" suddenly questioned Susan, wheeling round on Binkie.

"We haven't a garden," said Binkie, meeting the attack squarely; "but Father might let me have a red-and-white fuchsia out of one of the tubs or window-boxes."

"This garden wants a red-and-white fuchsia more than anything," said Susan.

Her voice was so friendly and nice that Binkie stared at her in surprise. Susan looked back, and the expression in her eyes was just as it had been at the end of that set. Then she smiled outright, and, taking out the mouth-organ, began to play the funny little tuneless tune.

CHAPTER IX

An Aspidistra and an Accident

Life, thought Binkie as she dressed next morning, is a surprising and complicated business. It would have been most simple and delightful if Rose Seymour's sister had gone into IIIA and had been received enthusiastically by Rose Seymour's adorers. Instead of that, the only girl she liked particularly was the only one Rose seemed particularly to dislike, and the form she was in waged perpetual war with IIIA. Binkie wondered if she should tell Rose that she thought Susan was going to be nice, and that she meant to throw in her fortunes with those of her own form, poor as they might be. Perhaps sometime. Not now. Not this morning, as, the condition of the manicure scissors having been discovered, there was a certain tension in the atmosphere, and Binkie had plenty of opportunity to meditate on life undisturbed by conversation or comment from Rose.

When she went into the form-room that morning she was astonished by the sight of Susan tidying up. The alder catkins were in the waste-paper basket, the aspidistra was in a pan of water, Susan was in a state of dishevelment, and there was a small clay jar of red and white daisies on Miss Loraine's desk.

"She'll upset them," Susan was saying to Mona Manders, who surveyed the scene with detached and spectacled complacency. "But you, being top and in the front row, will be the very person to swab up."

"Oh, shall I?" inquired Mona Manders, quite unshaken. "You think yourself very clever, Susan."

"And what is more, so I am," rejoined Susan. "And so is Binkie Seymour."

Binkie noticed that for the first time Susan had recognized her as herself, and not as "Rose Seymour's sister".

"Come and sponge the aspy," suggested Susan, with an ingratiating smile, as she plunged the blackboard duster into the pan of water and gently touched a dust-grimed leaf with it.

"Can't we scrap the aspy altogether?" asked Binkie. "It won't be nice even when it's clean."

"It's alive," said Susan. "And it has leaves." She was suddenly serious, looking at it.

"It's so ugly," said Mona, seeing a chance to side against Susan. They quite liked one another, but each thought the other an ass.

"So are many things in this world," said Susan, with point, "and yet they are allowed to live."

"They don't look so bad washed," Binkie hurried to say. She wanted Susan to do something friendly with her, not to waste time bickering with Mona.

"M-m-m-m. I'm not so sure about *that*," said Susan, looking thoughtfully at Mona. "I know!"—she suddenly forgot her victim in the pleasure of the inspiration. "We'll give it to IIIA, with love and best wishes. They'll be simply delighted with it."

"Will they?" said Mona, who was literal-minded. "*I* should say they'll be simply furious."

"Furious? With our pretty present?" Susan looked aghast. "Remember, it isn't the actual *value*, Mona, it's the *spirit* that counts."

"That's just the point," said Binkie.

Susan looked at her, with a little giggle.

"Help me to push in the old thing, Binks," she said. "It would be healthier to do it before Miss Squire arrives. No, we won't take it down that passage. There's a door opening into IIIA—this side."

There was. IIIB and IIIA knew that door pretty thoroughly. Mistresses strictly prohibited the opening of the fanlight, and the glass upper panels had been thoughtfully obscured with maps, maps which, however, were often thrust aside to allow looks of scorn, wondering pity, or contemptuous defiance to be exchanged. The door was always locked—and neither Miss Squire nor Miss Loraine knew there was a key. Had they known, Miss Squire would have had it. As they did not, there was a constant struggle for its possession. At present IIIB had it, and kept it secreted in the welter of Susan's desk—certainly the best hiding-place that could have been found. "But I know my way about in it," Susan would say with pride, and it was certainly rather wonderful to see the ease with which she drew out any required object. Had her effects been arranged with business-like order and method she could not have whipped out the key more quickly. As she fitted it into the lock, Binkie seized the large plant in a difficult embrace and staggered towards the door.

"We'll just put it down by their bowl of daffodils," said Susan, with a wicked chuckle; "they'll set it off so well."

Unfortunately Binkie and Susan put it down sooner than they had expected to do. Moving with some difficulty, and as much speed as they could, they collided with two indignant IIIA's, who, hearing the key turn, had at once sprung to the door, anticipating trouble. The four met in a sort of deadlock, like an agonized quartette in the "visiting" figure of lancers, complicated by the large solemn aspidistra waving in their midst.

"What's that?"

"It's for you."

"Take it back!"

"Don't you like it?"

"We simply won't have it."

"Oh, it's all right, really. Go on. Have it. We don't mind. We can easily get another."

"Don't be an ass, Susan. Take it back."

"Oh, don't be so *rude*. You're hurting my feelings. A nice way to accept a pretty present!"

"*Take it back!*"

"Get *out*, or we'll jolly well make you."

So went the conversation of the quartette, strengthened by violent pushings of the IIIA's, who were determined that the aspidistra should not adventure beyond the first line of desks. Binkie, half scared and half amused, saw Susan's impish face and the angry eyes of the IIIA's, and gripped the big, round, smooth, slippery, yellow pot as firmly as she could. But it was not firmly enough. The pressure of the opposing forces was too much for her; her aching arms suddenly relaxed, and, with a terrifying smash and a slide and thud of earth, the pot fell to the floor. The quartette, suddenly drawn together by the common bond of horror, stared at the mess. And at that moment there was the rustle of a gown, and the hawk lady, sharp and cool and alert, swooped down upon them.

"*What—?*" she inquired. She used one-third of the words any other mistress would have done, and she was more alarming than any except Edmund Ironsides herself.

The four looked up at her: Binkie and Susan in guilty and apologetic discomfort, the IIIA's in a glow of virtuous indignation.

"We didn't want it, Miss Squire!" cried one. "It's *their* aspidistra—their old aspidistra."

"We were trying to keep it out," said the other.

"M-m-m!" Miss Squire surveyed the shattered warrior. "Success not conspicuous."

Binkie glanced secretly at Susan, hoping that she might invent an amusing impudence which would float them off the rock on which they seemed to have run, but Susan had nothing to say. She knew, as Binkie learned afterwards, that the hawk lady would have gone one better.

"Dangerous neighbours," went on Miss Squire. "Must ask your form mistress to keep you under special control. An order mark apiece will probably bring you before her notice. Meanwhile—dustpan and brushes from the kitchen, please. And quickly. I cannot teach in a dust-heap."

Binkie gave a gasp. Miss Squire, looking at her with severity, thought it occasioned by disgust at clearing up, but it really came from the mere vision of the hawk lady on a dust-heap. In silence she accompanied Susan to the kitchen, where an irritating housemaid in a pink dress gave them what they asked for, with a grin. In silence the two returned to the classroom, and, quiet and cowed, set about the business of clearing up. It wasn't pleasant. Binkie withdrew the aspidistra and laid it out on a newspaper with solicitude, as if it were a rare and much-prized specimen. She hated it bitterly, but she somehow felt it necessary to do everything carefully under the hawk lady's eye. Susan, with a sort of reverence, as if she had been in church, gently coaxed bits of china and clods of earth into the dustpan. IIIA, by now seated in their places, stared with unsmiling amazement and curiosity. The hawk lady stood behind her desk, very still and rigid. Most of the time she too fixed her gaze on Binkie and Susan; once or twice she suddenly averted it and contemplated her blotting-pad.

"I can't get up this bit," said Susan at last. She had emptied her first contribution into Binkie's newspaper and was patiently and unavailingly trying to coax or surprise one thin strip of mould over the rim of the patent dustpan.

"A bit of thin paper would do it," cried Binkie.

"You may count that done," conceded Miss Squire.

Simultaneously with the deliverance of these two pieces of advice Susan swished her brush backwards and forwards, scattering the remnant of dust to the draughts of IIIA.

"These things are a test of character," commented Miss Squire. "It is doubtful, Susan, whether you will ever be anything so useful as a housemaid, but you have grasped the principles."

IIIA smiled. Susan went out of the room trying to carry her dustpan and brush with haughty dignity. She did not succeed. Binkie, following her, bearing the parcel of aspidistra in both arms, a dab of mould on one cheek, was a more noticeable failure. As soon as they were in the corridor they heard the uncontrolled amusement of IIIA. Susan spun round and looked furiously at the door.

"They shall pay for this," she said dramatically. "A hundred per cent interest, too. You'll see."

"Oh, don't do anything for a bit," implored Binkie.

"I won't," said Susan darkly. "Revenge won't spoil with keeping. The beggars! If we *did* push, they pulled. It took push *and* pull to do it."

"They looked so pleased with themselves," said Binkie, remembering the smiles with which they had watched Susan's manipulation of the dustpan.

"Didn't they? But they'll see. It's a long worm that has no turning."

Unable and unwilling to dispute this zoological fact, Binkie looked sympathetic.

"They're very cock-a-hoopish. They think they'll get everything. But we'll win something from them, Binks. We *must*."

"What can we win, though?"

Susan checked off possibilities with surprising speed.

"Gardens—we're out of that. Form—no, we haven't enough brain. Cricket—IIIB can't run. Tennis—it can't play. Swimming—swimming—Binkie, we'll have the swimming shield."

"But *can* IIIB swim?"

"You can. I can. That's two. We'll teach some more. If they won't learn, so much the worse for them."

Susan looked so fierce that Binkie felt quite alarmed, but she liked the "we".

"Right," she said in a soothing tone. "Anyway," she added whimsically, with a little pat of the newspaper parcel, "anyway, we *have* got rid of the aspidistra."

CHAPTER X

A Disastrous Afternoon

For a few days Miss Loraine seemed more than ever vague and melancholy, and Binkie felt sadly responsible, though Susan refused to acknowledge that she might be worrying over IIIB.

"It's the aspy, I expect," she said. "People nourish secret passions for the strangest things. She used to look at it a great deal. Now I dare say she can't remember the date of Magna Charta without it."

"I don't believe it," said Binkie. "She has simply fallen into one of her moods. She has probably forgotten about the form garden, and won't remember till she goes down in June to cut roses, and discovers there's nothing else there."

"Never mind. When we get the swimming shield that will wake her to reality," said Susan.

"Will it? I don't think she'll notice it till it has been hanging on the wall for days and weeks. Then she'll take it for a trophy of Hereward the Wake, or someone like that. She won't connect it with us."

"IIIA will, though," said Susan.

Binkie nodded cheerfully. But on her first visit to the baths she inwardly wondered at the confidence of Susan, who never seemed to doubt the success of any enterprise on which she had set her heart. The sight of IIIB in the water was enough to dash the most sanguine hopes. Susan herself swam well, though she wasted a lot of energy in the great splashing lunges of her side stroke. She said that this method was adopted from motives of policy, as the noise bewildered her opponents, and made them slack through sheer breathless astonishment. The Lilian who played tennis with Binkie had come to school with a very dressy swimming costume which Susan declared she had picked up second-hand at Trouville or Venice on account of the Great War. Forced to adopt the regulation school garment, she languished on the brink of the baths, looking sadly at herself as if she were mourning past glories. Some of IIIB clung to the chains in the three feet end, shuddering and saying how cold it was; some went half-way down the steps and then asked Miss Loraine, who, with a captured and grief-stricken expression, was on duty, if they might get out now; some, intrepid and reckless of mien, gambolled in shallow water, splashing their necks, rubbing their ears, ducking as far as their chins and springing up again with noises like spouting sea-serpents. The last performance seemed to irritate Susan.

"Isn't it pathetic?" she said to Binkie, as they sat side by side on the diving-board, surveying their team. "The daring beggars! *Look* at that one! Mother's pride and joy."

"We don't look likely to win a shield, certainly," said Binkie, watching the lordly IIIA's disport themselves, not one in less than five feet of water.

"Oh, I don't know about that," said Susan. Then, with a sudden swing back to her former tone—"Mercy on us! What's *that?*"

Binkie's eyes followed Susan's fascinated gaze, and saw Mona Manders standing in water reaching to her waist, inflating, with a solemn and portentous expression, a pair of wings destined to support her solid form in aquatic exercise. She had not removed her spectacles—Susan said she slept in them, in case she should wake in the night and fail to see a point—and the light shone upon them, and on the big pale-yellow swelling bladders, and on Mona's puffed-out cheeks. Binkie suddenly choked, and let herself fall into the water. Susan immediately splashed in after her, and, swimming crookedly and gaspingly, they got themselves to the side. There they stopped and gripped the chains, helpless.

"It's awfully mean to laugh," Binkie managed to say between spasms. "She's really doing well. She's our only chance. Look!"

The sight of Mona carefully and correctly propelling herself across, borne up by the wings which had so ludicrously inadequate an appearance, opening and shutting her mouth at regular intervals, overcame Susan a second time.

"Oh, *what* is it?" she cried again.

"I think she's jolly good," said Binkie, who somehow felt it her duty to restrain Susan a little. "She's so careful."

"Oh, isn't she?

"I thought I saw a porpoise fat a-floundering in the sea;
    I looked again and saw it was M. Manders from IIIB;
    I said: 'You'll *never* learn to swim, but to watch you *is* a spree'."

Binkie gave a chuckle.

"All the same, we must consider her," she said. "If we manage to get in for the Form Shield, Lilian and Mona are the two that must swim in the team with you and me."

"Oh, we need only one. It's a three team."

"We must have a substitute in case of accidents."

"True. Come along then. Let's encourage them a little."

Susan dashed off down the bath, while Binkie, rather doubtful as to her methods of encouragement, followed her closely.

"Hurry up, Lilian. Get in. It's glorious," invited Susan, spinning in a whirlpool before the sad gaze of the only figure still on the brink.

"*Glorious!* It looks horrible."

"Don't be morbid. Come in. You're going to swim in the IIIB team, you know."

"I am *not*," said Lilian, more definite than Binkie had known she could be. "I couldn't."

"Couldn't? Nonsense! You're a *swimmer!* You could swim the Channel if you gave your mind to it."

Looking as if she rather thought she could, Lilian sat down and put one foot into the water.

"Hurrah!" Susan, exultant and quite unable to restrain her triumph, reared up and, seizing Lilian round the waist, dragged her right in. Followed the usual shriek, storm of coughing gulps, and recriminations. As soon as she had sufficiently recovered, Lilian made for the steps, and, with more haste than she had ever before been seen to display, mounted them and dashed into her box. Channel swimmer or not, she had had enough.

"What a pity!" Susan looked after her with genuine remorse. "You shouldn't hurry people. I hate to be dragged under myself."

"Do you?" Susan eyed Binkie in sudden amused anticipation.

"No," said Binkie quickly. "I mean, I used to hate it before I could swim."

"There's Mona. Cheerio, Mona! You'll never get on in that shallow water. Come up into the deep end and you'll soon find your feet."

"Just what she won't find," thought Binkie sympathetically, as she watched Mona, who, a little complimented by the friendly interest of one whose notice was generally somewhat scathing, carefully turned and began slowly to propel herself after the light dashing form of Susan.

Miss Loraine blew a whistle. Miss Loraine blowing a whistle always tickled Binkie. It was no short sharp summons, but as melancholy as a lapwing's call, and about as much of an incentive to instant action.

"Time, girls!" she announced in her rather nice sad voice.

IIIA at once swam to the side, for Miss Squire's girls always stopped what they had just been doing at any sort of summons, and most of IIIB followed them, for they were thoroughly glad time was up. But Susan lifted up her voice in entreaty.

"Just five minutes for us, Miss Loraine," she implored. "Binkie and I dress so quickly, and Mona wants to practise in the deep end."

Mona gave an astonished gurgle, but was too much engrossed in and exhausted by what she was doing to become articulate. Miss Loraine looked resigned, and was understood to have given permission.

"I'll race you, Binkie!" Susan was suddenly excited by the stretch of rocking green water, empty of girls. So was Binkie. It was glorious just to go on without waiting for anyone to get out of the way, and she loved pitting her strength against Susan. Forgetting Mona, who was still labouring on her course, the two turned, trod water for a second, and, with their biggest hardest strokes, dashed down towards the shallow end.

What happened next Binkie wished she knew. She could only remember a gulping cry, a splash, heads over the doors of boxes, the attendant hurrying up the side of the bath with a life-belt, herself and Susan suddenly wheeling round and staring across the wash they had made—and Miss Loraine, swimming to the steps in the deep end, while Mona Manders, tucked away under one arm, was swallowing more water than she had ever done at one time during her life, though she was doing her very best not to swallow any.

"Mona!" ejaculated Susan. "I had completely forgotten her. She must have burst those wings, or lost them, or something."

Binkie was feeling too guilty to say a word. Very soberly the two swam to the side, hoisted themselves up by the chains, and pattered along to where Miss Loraine, water streaming from her blue dress, her hair quite dry, was hauling Mona out, while the baths attendant posed with the life-belt, and an I-could-have-told-you-all-along-this-would-happen expression. For a minute no one said a word.

"Are you all right, Mona?" then inquired Susan, in the chastened voice of the visitor by the sick-bed.

Miss Loraine to the rescue

Mona sneezed and spluttered and could say nothing. Binkie noticed that her spectacles were still on.

"Oh, *go* and get dressed," said Miss Loraine, wearily, squeezing water out of her skirt.

"Would you like to step into the hot-room, miss?" inquired the attendant, with a look of half-scathing pity. "It 'ud dry out the worst, and I'd lend you my mackintosh. I'd be pleased to lend it to you."

Miss Loraine, without enthusiasm, said how kind it was of the attendant, who was obviously despising her (*a*) for having let a girl get into difficulties, (*b*) for so speedily extricating her from them, and stepped into the hot-room. The attendant, who now meant to keep an eye on Mona till she was safely out of the building, followed her to her box. Susan and Binkie, with the mien of the guilty whom no one has yet reproached, returned to theirs.

Binkie peeled off her swimming-dress and gloomily enveloped herself in her bath sheet. The beginning of that afternoon had been great fun, but it seemed as if her luck were out. She wondered if, when Rose was twelve, she had managed to fall into a pond and break an aspidistra and be responsible for nearly drowning a Mona Manders, all in three days.

Then Susan's voice, still unusually awed and lowered, came from the next box.

"I say! Do you know that Miss Loraine has saved Mona Manders's life? It doesn't seem a bit like it, does it?"

"Oh, someone would have got her out," said Binkie quickly. "If she had shouted or whistled we should have got up in time."

"It was rather nice of her to go right in like that without waiting for anyone, though," said Susan.

"So it was. She looked annoyed when she got out too, as if she felt an ass."

Binkie, though she did not know it, had gauged the feelings of Miss Loraine, as she stood steaming in the hot-room, with great accuracy. She was wondering why these stupid things always happened to her, what she ought to have done, and what Miss Squire would look when she heard the story. Miss Squire would have had Mona out without getting wet herself—but then, had Miss Squire been on duty, Mona would not have been in after time was up.

"I wish Miss Loraine wasn't so wet," said Susan, after a short pause. "I wish I hadn't asked Mona up to the deep end. I suppose it was rather an idiotic thing to do."

"It was, rather," said Binkie honestly. "Don't mind, Susan. It has ended all right, and you won't do it again."

"No, I shan't," said Susan emphatically. "There'll be a tremendous row when we get back to school. I expect IIIB will be out of the swimming now. There's really no luck about IIIB."

Slowly and soberly putting on her shoes and stockings, Binkie felt that Susan was right.

CHAPTER XI

SUSAN IN TROUBLE

Astonishingly little more was heard of the episode. Miss Loraine said nothing about it at all. IIIB, encouraged by Binkie and Susan, said that this was the reticence of a heroine; IIIA, although it generally contradicted IIIB on principle, actually believed this too. Both forms had been impressed by the quickness and efficiency of Miss Loraine's life-saving, and they began to listen really attentively to the doings of England under Saxon and Norman kings. Miss Loraine did not think of attributing this phenomenon to her rescue of Mona Manders; she hardly realized it; she only knew that she was not so tired as usual in third-form history periods, and supposed that she must be getting used to them. As for Mona Manders, she blossomed forth in a new guise. Her spectacles shone with enthusiasm as she related, to anyone in IIIB who would listen, the story of her sensations as she went under water. In reality she could remember nothing but a feeling which combined a terrible choking-fit with a violent cold in the head, and then the sharp dig of Miss Loraine's elbow as she seized her; but she had read enough drowning stories to know what one should undergo in such circumstances. "As the water closed round me, all the events in my past life flashed through my brain in a moment of time," she would say. Watching Susan during these narratives, Binkie would feel sorry for her; for Susan's sense of decency wouldn't let her rag a person who had been nearly drowned through her fault, and she would listen with an expression of pained and strained attention, and make polite ejaculations of wonder and sympathy, which came as oddly from her as the behaviour of a bishop's wife at afternoon tea would

from Puck. The only compensation was Mona's prowess at the
baths. Far from alarming her, the episode seemed to have put new
enthusiasm into her. She regarded the water as her own special
sphere, and, with a resolute gesture, discarded the faithless wings.
With an expression of do-or-die determination and unshakable
complacency she practised in the four-feet water, first swimming
three strokes to the chains, then half across the baths, then right
across. On all these occasions Binkie and Susan swam with her,
one on either side. It was one of the few sights that made Miss
Loraine, bored with supervision, smile; but they were far too
anxious and too much engrossed to notice her entertainment.
Mona might be relied upon to swim for the shield—though
whether she would be of any real help was doubtful. That IIIB
must enter for the shield, and, even if they did not win it, defeat
IIIA for a place in the finals, Binkie and Susan were agreed. The
superiority of IIIA was maddening. Every week, when their
perfect record was read in hall by Miss Edmund, they radiated
satisfaction, increased though suppressed as they listened to the
doubtful one of IIIB which followed. Their manners were too
good for open exultation when Miss Squire was there; when she
wasn't they became primitive. They said that IIIB couldn't do
G.C.M. sums; that IIIB didn't know the names of their relations
in French; that IIIB thought Cairo was in North America; that
IIIB was still reading out of a primer about fat cats who sat on
mats; that IIIB couldn't learn passages from Shakespeare and
had been put back to "The Boy stood on the Burning Deck",
"Master Tommy Rook", and "The Spider and the Fly". IIIB
was powerless against this invective. It could not hurl back the
favourite accusation—"You're swots. *We* are sports," for IIIA was
good at games. It could not point out the advantages of beauty
versus brains, for IIIA was a handsome form. It sometimes said:
"Think yourself very clever, don't you?" to which IIIA rejoined:
"We do"; or "Funny, aren't you?" to which IIIA instantly agreed:
"We are." There was no way of getting at them—nothing would

be of any avail except defeating them publicly. And the only chance was in the swimming match.

"Don't let them know how good we are," Susan would say to Binkie, too much in earnest to be humble. "Let them think that Mona Manders is our star turn." To this strategy Binkie consented. So she and Susan played about together or escorted Mona on her ventures on Tuesdays, when IIIA was there; on Fridays, when they bathed with Form V, they spent their whole half-hour doing lengths at top speed, while Miss Loraine, by special request, timed them and coached them. Miss Loraine was beginning to like them. They had tidied their room, and they kept the glasses filled with fresh flowers. They disciplined IIIB in an extraordinarily efficient manner, and no one dared sharpen her pencil on the floor. In rain or sunshine they worked at the garden, which they obviously loved, and they loved the things Miss Loraine gave them for it. She began to think that small girls are not so bad when you get to know them. With one of her bursts of energy she took down the depressing pictures from her form-room walls, extracted them from their frames, and put in some gloriously brightly-coloured prints of scenes from mediæval history. Binkie and Susan, mounted on desks, helped to hang them, and no one, not even Miss Loraine, broke glass or spilt ink. They had parrot tulips sent from Susan's home, for decoration that week, and their room was so gay with the new prints and the great gaudy flowers that Miss Edmund said it was a pleasure to teach Scripture in it, and the glances of IIIA pausing by the door changed from scorn to wonder. They recovered, and said that the tulips looked artificial and that the history pictures were a kindergarten series for which Miss Loraine had been obliged to send post-haste to London, to teach IIIB a little about their period before the examinations, but they had been impressed, and Binkie and Susan knew it.

Binkie knew rather more of IIIA than anyone else, for Myra and Cecil, though they joined in the mob cry against IIIB as a whole, were always polite and friendly if they met her singly, and even sought her out, for they could not forget that she was the sister of the beloved Rose. Of Rose herself Binkie now saw very little. She had the prefect's privilege of sleeping out on the balcony above the cloisters, and as the girls who availed themselves of it were supposed to use the room next the balcony for dressing and undressing she had "moved" temporarily, and Binkie had the dignity of a small dormitory to herself. She was sorry in a way: she wanted to let Rose know that IIIB wasn't as bad as she thought, that she had misjudged Susan in particular; and Rose couldn't be convinced of a thing like that in a hasty few minutes' conversation. There would be no chance of the misunderstanding being put right till Rose really got to know Susan. That would be, Binkie thought, when the prefects' teas began.

These festivities were considered by the juniors to be the best of the year. They began in June, and took place on Saturdays. Then the Sixth entertained the younger girls in rotation, beginning with the First and ending with the Third. During the winter the Fourth and Fifth entertained the Sixth. Sometimes the prefects' party was a strawberry feast; sometimes a hay picnic; sometimes an excursion to a ruined abbey or church with tombs of crusaders in it; or to a castle with a moat and a dungeon. Juniors are catholic in their tastes; and, whether invited to contemplate the marble effigies of cross-legged knights and ladies with stiffly folded gowns, or to bury one another in the sweet brownish hay threaded with fading buttercups and daisies, or to search Brackleigh Woods for the little wild strawberries with the exciting taste, the guests enjoyed themselves to ecstasy. Binkie had heard much of these entertainments, and she wanted to go out for the day with IIIB and the prefects, with Susan and Rose. She believed that directly these two came face to face at a party they must like one another: Rose was so clever and pretty and wonderful; Susan so funny and amusing and nice, and so good a friend. Never, since that bewildering morning when she had pushed Binkie into the housemaid's cupboard, had she gone back on her, and, although Binkie was not old enough to know much about the behaviour of friends, somehow she felt sure that she could trust this one.

Meanwhile Susan did not think much about Rose. Although, as Myra and Cecil had said, she had a quick temper, it soon spent itself, and she enjoyed life too much to cherish grievances. Working in the garden with Miss Loraine and Binkie, seeing it come right again and look more charming than it ever had done, gave her so much pleasure that she forgot the bulb squabble and its disastrous results. Sparring with IIIA was enough outlet for other energies, and the fight that she and Binkie meant to put up for the swimming shield satisfied ambition. Because she was happy, Susan had the appearance of a reformed character, and even the prefects forgot that she had been a nuisance. But Fate, which never was to let her alone for long, did not intend that this peace should continue.

Friendly as she now was with Binkie, Susan never wanted to be with anyone all the time. She meant to go round the world by herself when she grew up; at present she was confined to solitary wanderings about the garden and the field with the brook that belonged to St. Helen's. When she was in the field she was generally very quiet, for she knew that anyone walking quiet and alone sees and hears wee beasts and birds who become silent or scurry into hiding if friends walk and talk together. But in the garden she went jauntily, playing the little tuneless tune on her mouth-organ. The calm with which the juniors accepted this habit was proof of the strength with which her personality asserted itself. No one, not even the most ribald of IIIA, commented on it. If they had been working for public examinations or scholarships they probably would have said something; as they were not, Susan remained in happy ignorance of the fact that her music might be a powerful irritant. It was not natural wickedness, but mere bad luck, that brought her to the sunny balustrade that bounded the terrace outside the prefects' study window. Propped against a short pillar, legs stretched out along the parapet, hair a little ruffled, Susan played her mouth-organ. Whether it was the influence of the sunny rose-scented afternoon, or of the direct example of a little stone Pan who held up a hoof to dance to his pipes at the top of the flight of steps leading from the terrace to the lower garden, she excelled herself, giving a performance of far greater variety than was usual. She played one or two bars of popular melodies *prestissimo*, as if afraid that she would forget if she stopped to think; and these beginnings were intercepted by a slow rendering of her own odd little tune. The effect was indescribable. Lesley Crawford and Rose, at work on either side of the table, at a particularly stiff bit of Tacitus, at first moved uneasily. Then they clapped their hands to their heads. Then they stared at one another in irritated despair. Then Lesley Crawford got up and stamped to the window, while Rose fluttered the leaves of her dictionary extra quickly, as if the effort might drown the sound outside.

"Oh, it's a *child*," said Lesley, as if she had expected a young dragon to have crawled from one of the gate-posts to serenade the Sixth. "That wretched child Susan Crashaw."

"That explains it," said Rose irritably. "I can't bear that child. Speak to her, Lel. Tell her she can't stop here."

It was a pity that Lesley did the telling, rather than Rose, or Rhoda Tyndale, who was so courteous a young woman that no junior could refuse instantly to do as she desired. Lesley never compromised, never spared anyone's feelings—in fact, she would not have granted that a junior had feelings. She addressed them in the quick curt tone of an efficient puppy-trainer. Some of them, who were indeed rather like puppies, did not object to this, and served Lesley with small-girl devotion; others, among whom was Susan, immediately became thorny when she addressed them.

"What d'you think you're doing?" inquired Lesley.

Susan turned up an innocent face, and, fixing a dreamy grey gaze on Lesley, gave a few bars of "Comin' thro' the Rye".

"Mad?" asked Lesley. "If you want to play that errand-boy instrument, why not learn to do it? Sounds as if it had hiccups or something."

Insulted as an artist, Susan removed the instrument from her mouth.

"It's you that hear in hiccups," she said. "You simply have no music in you."

She went on with the tuneless tune. Rose, exasperated, got up and came to the window.

"Please stop doing that, Susan," she said. "We can't work."

Because there was some point in this; also because Rose was Binkie's sister, Susan was prepared to obey. Rose would have let the matter end there, but Lesley could never resist following up a victory.

"And just hand over that horrid mouth-organ," she said. "We are not going to run the risk of being worried with it again."

Susan immediately put her precious instrument in her pocket. She enjoyed it so much that she had always expected it to be confiscated, and she did not intend to give it up without a struggle.

"It's an 'Echo'," she pointed out in a hurt voice.

"You shall have it back in the hols.," said Lesley. "But bring it over here in double quick time, or you won't get it then."

Susan smiled pleasantly, shaking her head. Both Rose and Lesley felt natural exasperation.

"Oh, well, if you don't choose to *bring* it."

Lesley vaulted out of the window, crossed the grass, and before the astonished Susan had time to slide from the parapet, or even to protect her property, she found herself pinned to the hard stone coping, while Lesley's muscular hand closed on hers. At once she struggled and clawed like a little tiger-cub, but it was useless. Lesley was not hockey and cricket captain for nothing, and Susan knew she had not a chance against her. This conviction made her temper fiercer, and Lesley, though sure of victory, found her difficult to deal with.

"Rose! Rose!" she shouted. "Come and lend a hand. Get hold of the thing while I keep her down."

It was not very dignified, but a prefect must be backed up, and Rose, after a second's hesitation, lowered herself from the study window and ran to Lesley's assistance. In a minute her strong cool fingers had loosened the small ones clasped round the shining tin, and the exasperated Susan knew that she had been defeated. She could have cried with rage. Wildly she began to stammer out something, but she was too angry to be articulate and the words would not come.

"Too full for sound or foam," said Lesley. "Let's tip her over the parapet, and send her a longer way round."

Lesley was afraid that Susan, ignoring all respect due to a prefect, would seize her skirt and slide back with her to the study, insisting with ferocity that her instrument should be returned. Although surer of her position than Lesley, Rose perhaps thought the same thing. The two took Susan very gently in their arms, and, as if they were handling an inestimable treasure, lowered her across the parapet into a tuft of long grass and fool's-parsley. Then they returned to their work, leaving her to her own thoughts.

For a few minutes these were unfit to chronicle. The loss of the mouth-organ was bad enough; the sense of powerlessness and complete defeat was worse. It would have been a relief to Susan if she could have opened her mouth wide and howled like a baby. As this was impossible, she squirmed in the grass and fool's-parsley, tearing up big handfuls of it, digging the toes of her shoes into tangles near the earth. Then she clutched an early nettle, was badly stung, and felt better. She got up, licking her hurt hand, and glared at the half-open window of the prefects' study. Her thoughts, churned into an angry indistinguishable mass, began to settle themselves.

One thing she resolved—she would get back that mouth-organ. The prefects thought themselves very clever—they should just see.

CHAPTER XII

Of all this Binkie was quite ignorant. She was so happy that she did not notice anything wrong with her friend, who was subject to moods, but who emerged from them so quickly and completely that it was not worth while to hurry her. While Rose and Lesley were tipping Susan into the fool's-parsley she had been working with Miss Loraine in the form garden, which seemed to her the loveliest thing she had known. She understood now what her father had meant by ready-made flowers. She could not have guessed that blue such as that of delphinium and larkspur could have been in anything tangible, like a petal, in anything but blue sky, or that a thing so delicate and gay as a columbine could grow out of earth with worms in it. (Although she was always to love gardens, Binkie could not get used to worms.) And when the roses began to come she could hardly believe they were real. Not only was the garden endless pleasure and excitement, but she liked her work, and because she was interested in it, and did it well, the others began to wonder if there might not be more in books than they had thought. Before this any capacity for getting marks had been associated in their minds with the uninspired carefulness of Mona Manders; Binkie worked gaily, as if it were fun, and it was certainly interesting to hear her read aloud. Quite unconsciously they all began to quicken; but Binkie little dreamed that every mistress who taught IIIB taught it rather better because she was there. She just went on, forgetful of her first qualms, finding everything very good fun.

Only she missed Rose a little. Their play-hours were at different times, and Rose had warned her that she had better keep clear of the prefects' study. She would not have seen her until the Sixth entertained IIIB if it had not been for her birthday, which came during the last week in June. Then, directly after breakfast, she went shyly across to the prefects' study, carrying a translation of the tragedies of Euripides. She had not herself hit upon the idea of giving this as a present; she had consulted her mother, who was always furnished with a list of her elder daughter's requirements, for Rose did not believe in taking risks, and would not pretend pleasure if she did not like a thing. She rarely had presents she did not want, and, if she missed the delight, she also avoided the annoyance that a complete surprise can give.

"Just what I should have chosen," she declared, as she solemnly unwrapped and examined the green book, and kissed the top of Binkie's head. "And how are you getting on, Binks?"

With the comforting lack of modesty possible when speaking to relatives, Binkie told Rose that she was getting on splendidly, and then wandered round the room, examining its contents with the curiosity of the small girl. Rose had a bookcase to herself, and it was filled with books bright to see and pleasant to hold. Lesley, who was doing science, had several glass bowls and jars full of intriguing creatures which wriggled or darted or floated; Rhoda Tyndale was making a big relief map of the St. Helen's district. Rose had sketched out a picture history chart for Miss Loraine, to assist in the instruction of Form I, and meant to finish it in the last three weeks of July, when the scholarship exam. would be over. This chart fascinated Binkie: it made her feel so clever. "Battle of Senlac or Hastings, 1066," she announced, staring at the diagram of a thin Norman and stout Saxon fighting a sort of stage duel. "And there's the Doomsday Book, like a big Bible. ... And William Rufus with an arrow stuck through him. What a face! He looks as if he were seriously hurt. What are those two roses? Are you going to put them there for your signature, right in the middle?"

"Think again, my child. There are two, you will observe: a red one and a white one."

"Oh yes. The. Wars of the Roses. But they don't look as if they were fighting. They're linked together as if they were friends."

"You're mistaken. They're locked in deadly combat. Now, what's that?"

Rose unrolled her chart a little farther to display a realistic and highly-coloured portrait of an explosion.

"That's Queen Elizabeth in a rage," said Lesley's voice from the deep arm-chair by the fire-place. "Or Shakespeare hatching a tragedy."

"It's the Gunpowder Plot," said Binkie reprovingly. "1605. It's a beautiful chart, Rose."

Rose smiled, spreading it out on the low table by the window.

"I might do a bit of it to-day," she said. "It's too near the exam. for work. ... Thank you very much for the Euripides, Binks. Oughtn't you to be back in your form-room now?"

With one lingering covetous glance at a newt in a jar, Binkie took herself off. Lesley told Rose what a good child her sister was, well-trained and all that; they both said that it was a pity she was in IIIB, and then, collecting their books, they sauntered off to their form-room for the day's work.

Rose's birthday was a Wednesday, and Wednesday was a full day for the Sixth. A scrambled lunch was followed by special coachings for scholarship and matriculation candidates, who then rushed down to the baths to cool their brains and refresh their bodies by a short swim before tea. It was not till after five o'clock that Lesley Crawford returned to the study with a jam-jar, to collect certain poly-wogs wanted as a loan exhibit to the Second. At first she noticed nothing amiss. She went straight to the window-sill where her creatures lived in their big glass bowls, and, making a hollow of her hand, began to scoop up the choicest. Then Rose came in, and Lesley, turning to communicate a bit of gossip overheard at the baths, saw a sight which made her gasp and drop her largest tadpole. Rose had seen it already, and the two crossed to her window and stood staring at it in bewilderment, anger, and dismay.

The chart still lay spread out where Rose had left it after showing it to her sister, but the symbolic pictures which had delighted Binkie were no longer visible. A thick brown substance with a piquant smell had spread itself over the neat bright work. Bits of broken glass stuck up here and there, and half a bottle with a green label lay on its side. Near it was a twist of blue ribbon, half holding two beautiful roses, a "Liberty" and "Bride". Small wonder that the two girls stared for a moment in perfect silence. Then Lesley opened her mouth.

"What—on—earth—?" she began.

"Oh, Lesley, *do* pick up that tadpole," said Rose in rather a strained voice.

People nearly always obeyed Rose, and Lesley at once dropped on her knees, and, after a short and noisy search, discovered the squirming and exhausted adventurer, and put him back in the bowl. Then she returned to Rose, who had extracted a card from the mess on the table, and was staring at it in new bewilderment. Lesley read over her shoulder.

"'To Rose Seymour, with grateful admiration, on her eighteenth birthday," she enunciated. "Many happy returns, and may all your tomorrows be as bright as to-day!"

Rose gave a little sad laugh.

"A funny man, evidently, whoever it was," she said.

"With enough sense not to risk handwriting," snarled Lesley, examining the staggering print. "And whatever—"

She picked up the broken bottle.

"Superfine Mango Chutney. ... As supplied to the House of Lords. ... What—? And here's a bottle of piccalilli. It's not broken, only cracked."

Rose fished out the blue ribbon and the perfect roses.

"There's no doubt that this is a birthday present," she said, "from someone who really rather hates me."

"Hates *you?*" Lesley was incredulous.

"Yes—don't you see? Pickles and vinegar: funny allusion to

my bitter ways. Haven't you yet heard the good old encrusted jokes about vinegar bottles and pepper pots? Well—this is the same notion, only rather messier."

She looked at her chart, and looked away rather quickly. It wasn't a very grand or wonderful or intellectual piece of work; it wasn't to be entered for a prize competition or school show; but it had been fun doing it, and Miss Loraine would have had fun showing it to the small ones. Binkie's enjoyment of it had proved that Form I would like it.

Lesley blazed.

"*Funny!*" she cried. "I jolly well wish I could get hold of the person or persons who did it. Their sense of humour would be considerably refined by the time I had finished with them. You'll see. ... I suppose it is utterly spoiled, Rose? Hold on a sec. I'll get my sponge."

She flew off to the balcony dorm. and returned with her sponge: a new one, bigger than her head, and greatly valued and cherished by its owner, who washed it constantly in soapless water lest it should get slimy, and exposed it to the sun to preserve its beautiful light yellow colour. She now smacked the treasure incontinent on the mess, cleaning off smears of chutney and prickles and splinters of broken glass. Rose looked on, touched.

"Don't ruin your sponge, Lel dear," she said. "There's no sense in that. The chart is done for, anyhow. I'll do another after the schol. I shan't get it finished before the end of term, but it'll be just as useful to Miss Loraine next year."

"When you won't be here to know how the children like it," growled Lesley. "And Miss Loraine will get married or something like that in the summer. She won't want a history chart then."

"True," said Rose. "Well, no use to fuss now. Got a newspaper, Lel? Let's push all this mess out of sight. Except the roses—we'll keep them. I'll take off the outside petals, and they will be all right."

"Oh, Rose, throw the beastly things away. They're insults."

"They're nothing of the sort. I don't care what they were meant to be. They're lovely in themselves, and no one can spoil them. I shall put them in water just now, and wear them at supper to-night."

"Coals of fire, I suppose. Well, you must go your own way, but you're wrong. They're probably full of electric snuff. That's the sort of thing this wag would consider funny."

"They're all right. Don't say anything to the others, Lel. There's no point in it."

"There's an extremely obvious point in it! I'm not going to let this affair rest, Rose. It's an outrage, mean and hateful, and whoever did it shall jolly well suffer for it."

"Oh, well, don't say anything to-night. I want to enjoy to-night. ... It's so much horrider to have that sort of thing done to you if other people know about it. When they don't, it doesn't seem so real, and in time you come to think you have read about it in a book."

Lesley stared at Rose.

"Well, you're beyond me," she said. "But have it your own way. It's your birthday, and you have certain rights. ... I'm awfly sorry about it," she added gently.

"I know you are," said Rose. "Wash that old sponge of yours, or you'll spoil your beauty with a piece of glass."

Lesley took the sponge, walked towards the door, and suddenly stopped short. Then she dashed to her table, pulled out a drawer, and felt right to the back of it.

"Gone!" she exclaimed dramatically. "I knew it."

"Knew what? What has gone?"

"That wretched child's mouth-organ. It was there last night. I knew she would come in and sneak it. She is responsible for that mess, Rose."

Rose's face hardened.

"It's exactly the sort of thing she would do. Pickles and roses, and 'may all your to-morrows be as bright as to-day'. I'd recognize that touch anywhere."

Rose was silent.

"Well, now we've got her," said Lesley with satisfaction. "And now we'll jolly well deal with her. There won't be much spirit left in that young woman after this next encounter."

"Oh, leave her alone," said Rose.

"*What?*" Lesley stared at Rose with surprise that was almost exasperation.

"We don't *know*, after all. It's only circumstantial evidence."

"Circumstantial evidence! Rose! You do think it's Susan. Don't you?"

"Yes, I suppose I do," confessed Rose. "But still—"

"But still what?" Lesley was nearly at the end of her patience.

"Well—I believe Binkie is rather fond of Susan. I've seen them out together a lot lately."

"In that case, the sooner Binkie knows what sort of young bounder Susan is the better."

"Oh, I don't know."

"Rose! This is sheer raving sentimentality."

"No, it isn't," said Rose definitely. "I'm sick of IIIB. I simply don't want to have any more to do with them, or with Susan, who *is* IIIB. Nothing. We won't entertain them this year. Nothing need be said—we'll simply ignore them. I'm not going to be soft with them. We'll make it up to Binkie somehow. ... Perhaps I'll settle with Susan some time. Only I don't want a row just now. Leave it to me; there's a good old thing. After all, it *is* my affair."

"Right you are," grumbled Lesley. "But you want someone to manage your affairs. Mind, I'm only promising for to-night. If I get the opportunity of making that unspeakable little blighter pay for what she has done, I can't promise not to take it. I should only break my word."

CHAPTER XIII

LESLEY SPEAKS HER MIND

In spite of her warning, Lesley did do what Rose wished. She contented herself with hinting to the Sixth that there was something between IIIB and Rose; that the form had blackened its always dingy reputation; and that it was to be sent to Coventry. "Rose is a little upset," she told them confidentially. "She's sure to unburden her heart to you quite soon. But don't press her. Only, believe me, the thing to be done is to be simply unaware of IIIB. Don't rag them or anything of that sort; behave as if you didn't know there were such persons in the school."

The prefects believed Lesley, and, though curious to know what had taken place, were willing to wait until Rose should choose to tell them. They were ready to ignore IIIB, against whom they had many old grudges, almost forgotten since Binkie came to school and the form had mysteriously ceased to be a nuisance. At first IIIB did not notice their disgrace. Then Susan and Binkie offered to fag balls for Rhoda Tyndale and Clare Lucas, and were politely thanked and told that their services were not required. A few minutes later Myra and Cecil presented themselves and were accepted. Also, girls from Forms III were chosen to perform various services at the end-of-term matches and festivities, and not a IIIB name appeared in the lists the Sixth posted in the hall. Binkie, because she was sensitive, and Susan, because she felt guilty, were the first to observe these signs of disfavour. They said nothing, however, until Mona Manders hurried up to a group resting after tennis one evening. She was full of importance and dismay.

"Do you know that the Sixth have asked the II's to a strawberry tea?" she inquired.

"Well, why not?" Binkie wanted to know.

"Why not? It's our week. IIIA last week. And they have asked all the II's together, which looks as if they were hurrying over their entertainment, and meant to leave us out."

"Oh, they can't," said Lilian dismally, while all the IIIB girls showed signs of distress.

"Commem. is over, and we shan't have a decent thing to eat before the garden party, and that's a long time to look forward to."

"Can't be helped," said Susan. "They *do* mean to leave us out. I've noticed something nasty about them for a week. I thought I would overlook it, but I cannot let this pass."

They smiled at the mimicry of a favourite phrase of their last year's form mistress, but it was without much amusement. Apart from the fun and the good things to eat at the prefects' party, they felt that it was bitter to be left out, especially as they did not know the reason.

"Perhaps the IIIA's won't notice that *we* haven't been asked," said Binkie.

"Oh, *won't* they? They shouted something after me in the playground about naughty little girls not being allowed to go to the party, but I didn't know what they meant, so pretended that I didn't hear," said Susan.

"But what have we done?" Mona Manders swept the group with her spectacled gaze, as if someone might have the required information blazoned on her brows.

"Don't you know? Can't you ask Rose?" someone questioned Binkie. But Binkie shook her head.

"Rose has gone up to town to-day," she said. "I think she would have told me if there had been anything wrong. It must be a big thing, you know."

"Oh, that doesn't follow," said Susan, who was sharpening a pencil so carelessly that the lead broke again and again. "Little things annoy the Sixth. I don't mean Rose. Not Rose, Binks. You have brought her up properly, thank goodness. But the rest of them. Touchy! Uncontrolled!"

IIIB, with the exception of Binkie, looked with some suspicion at Susan, who, after a cut or two more at her pencil, got up, and, with extreme nonchalance, strolled away.

"I expect Susan has been cheeky," grumbled an individual not particularly renowned for courtesy. "If she has, I think we ought to complain, and point out to the Sixth that it's nothing to do with us. There's no reason why we should all suffer for one person. There's no reason why Susan should not be left out and the rest of the form asked."

Binkie had a steady temper, but this sort of thing made her blaze.

"I'd like to know where the rest of the form would be if it weren't for Susan?" she inquired. "Who slaves in the garden, and keeps the form-room nice, and plays tennis like a champion, and knows her irregular verbs like—"

Imagination failed to find a simile, though it was true that Susan had suddenly developed a passion for French irregular verbs. She always found exceptions easier than general rules, and, as some of the mistresses knew, was the sort of girl who might be called clever when she was in the Sixth.

"She only works in the garden because you do," said Lilian, who had liked Binkie since that fateful game of tennis. "You're the person who has done most for the form, Binks. It has been nicer ever since you came into it."

Overwhelmed, Binkie stared at Lilian for a few seconds. Then she collected her wits.

"Well, I don't want to go to any Sixth Form party unless Susan goes," she said definitely. "I don't believe that it is her fault that we have been left out. If the Sixth think she has done anything wrong, they are probably wrong themselves. There's no reason why they shouldn't be. They're only mortal."

With this incontestable truth, Binkie also strolled off. She was hurt and dismayed, afraid that the duel between Susan and Rose had been renewed, afraid that the outcome of it might be worse than she could guess. Hoping to find Susan, she went to the form garden. But Susan wasn't there, and, choosing a good way to still anxiety, she filled the three biggest watering-cans and began to drench the flower-beds.

Meanwhile Susan had resolved upon action. In spite of her unconcerned demeanour, she was much distressed by the latest manifestation of Sixth Form hostility. A treat was always a treat, and Lilian's statement was only too true. IIIB would have nothing exciting to eat before the garden party, and by then the strawberries would be over. She felt that if the truth came out IIIB would have a real grievance against her, and, although she cared for none of them but Binkie, she liked to be "right" with them. Surely she could pacify the Sixth—if she were ready and willing to consume large quantities of humble pie, IIIB might be allowed their long-expected feast of more desirable meats. Feeling oddly nervous, but resolved not to draw back, she sought the prefects' room.

At first she knocked so politely that she failed to make herself heard. Her second attempt was rather too loud, and the tone of Lesley's "Come in!" was not encouraging. However, firm of purpose, she opened the door and boldly entered.

Lesley was there alone, grating dog-biscuit to feed gold-fish. The look which she turned on the visitor might have made a warrior tremble. It unsteadied Susan a little, and with undignified haste she extracted the mouth-organ from her patch-pocket. It did not come out alone. A handkerchief with knotted corners, a penknife, three Chinese stamps, a reel of transparent sticking-paper, a packet of seeds, two J nibs, a penny, a smooth shining white stone, and a handful of crumbs came out too. Susan held the mouth-organ in her outstretched left hand, as, with still greater speed, she replaced these treasures with her right. Lesley simply stared at her and said nothing.

"I've brought this back," said Susan. "Keep it for ever if you want to."

Still Lesley did not say a word.

"Shall I put it back in the drawer?" Susan suggested. "That's where I found it."

"As you like," said Lesley.

For once in her life Susan looked helpless. She had not expected this, and did not know how to deal with it. But she would do the thing thoroughly now she had made up her mind to do it. She cast about in her mind for the largest slice of humble-pie she could find, and, having discovered it, began to gobble it without self-pity or self-mercy.

"I'm sorry I came and took it," she said. "I was awfully angry, and I did miss it so. I felt all wrong without it. I didn't know I was disturbing you that day—I forgot your window was there."

Raising her eyebrows, Lesley dug a sixpence into her grated dog-biscuit. Susan felt desperate.

"Look here—have you cut out IIIB because of me?" she said. "If so, please do ask them. I don't want to come."

Lesley looked at her coldly.

"Christian martyr?" she said. "I see."

The rejoinder that only if she were to accept an invitation from the Sixth would she count herself a martyr was on the tip of Susan's tongue, but she managed to keep it there. With unnatural concentration she watched Lesley scatter the grated biscuit on the calm surface of the water in the bowl, and the instant response of the foolish round-mouthed fish. Lesley took no notice of her, but, dusting the sixpence and slipping it into her pocket, turned as if to go out of the room. Then she stopped short.

"Please clear," she said. "It's time for my coaching class, and I can't leave you here alone."

Susan flushed.

"I don't think you ought to say that," she said, her voice

faltering a little. "I have brought back my mouth-organ, and I shan't take it again."

"Oh, bother your mouth-organ," said Lesley with sudden temper. "Take the silly thing back with you. We don't care whether you have it or not. Pursue your errand-boy amusements as much as you like, as long as you don't do it within our hearing."

Because she saw no sense in refusing it, Susan took the mouth-organ. Evidently it was useless to apologize to Lesley—nothing could be done for IIIB. Then she had a sudden inspiration.

"When is Rose Seymour coming back?" she asked.

Up to this point Lesley had kept her eyes averted from Susan; but now she looked at her fixedly.

"You want to see Rose Seymour, do you?" she asked. "You find you are not to have your annual feed, and you come cringing across here to tell Rose that you are sorry."

"I don't want to tell her that I am sorry," said Susan, with rising temper. "I haven't anything to be sorry for—I was sorry for taking back the mouth-organ, because I didn't want IIIB to be cut out of the entertainment. But *you* took it away from me, not Rose. I'd like to see Rose because she would probably give some reason for not asking IIIB. She wouldn't just stand and be superior and say nothing."

"Look here, my good child, if you're not careful I shall say something I'll be sorry for," said Lesley. "You can thank your lucky stars and Rose Seymour that you are not in rather serious trouble at present. A reason for *not* asking IIIB! Perhaps you'll go quietly away and think out a reason for *asking* IIIB—the worst form that has ever been in St. Helen's, and you are the worst girl in it. It isn't as if you were high-spirited and amusing—you do low-down things. I wish you'd clear out of this room. To tell you the truth, I simply can't bear the sight of you."

There are some things that people don't say, and Lesley, who prized good form, was dismayed to hear her own voice speaking one of them. But she was too angry to withdraw her words;

indeed, had she tried, it would have been impossible. Susan had heard many criticisms of herself in the course of her short life, but never had she felt a hurt like that inflicted by that quick spontaneous declaration of Lesley's. For she knew in herself that both Rose and Lesley mattered—although she had been angry when Rose misjudged her about the IIIA garden last spring, and when she had been tipped gently and ignominiously into that fool's-parsley bed a few days ago, she did not detest or despise either of them. Had she been in the wrong at present Lesley's outburst would have done her more good than any amount of quiet reasoning or drastic punishment. As it was, she gave Lesley a queer white look, opened the door, and went away.

Lesley, throbbing with indignation, got her books together with the clumsiness of temper. She dropped her pencil-case and a sheaf of scribbled notes: she knocked against her bowls and gave their inhabitants the experience of what a storm might be. She felt right and wrong, excited and thoroughly uncomfortable.

"It's because Rose is away," she thought with impatience. "I wish the week were over, and Rose were back again at school."

CHAPTER XIV

IIIB GETS ITS CHANCE

For the next few days, Binkie could not understand Susan. She wandered off alone more often than she usually did, and, when they were together, her moods changed with bewildering rapidity. One hour she would be scornful and detached, as she had been when Binkie first came into IIIB; the next she would be curiously gentle, as if she weren't well, and wanted someone to be particularly nice to her. And her spirits were dashed: she performed the secret swimming practices without any enthusiasm, and the loveliness of the IIIB garden, now at its best, did not provoke any pleasure. She let Binkie exult, which Binkie did, and assented listlessly, without interest, as if she didn't care for flowers, and had done no more work in the garden than the majority of IIIB.

"I say, Susan, is anything wrong?" Binkie had to ask, though she was still a little scared at Susan in a mood.

"No." Susan's mouth snapped tight. She liked Binkie more than she had ever liked anyone, and she had made up her mind not to let her know how she stood with Rose and Lesley— she was curiously and increasingly ashamed of their evidently unforgiving anger with her. "Why on earth should you think so?"

"Because you don't look a bit happy."

"Well, one can't grin like a Cheshire cat all the time."

Binkie saw that one could not, and was silent.

"I'm quite happy," went on Susan. "Only I'm sick of IIIB, and of school. I'll be glad when the holidays come."

"I shan't, altogether," said Binkie.

"Why?"

"I'll miss you so much when I go home."

Susan looked as startled as Binkie had done when Lilian had proclaimed her effect upon IIIB. For a second Binkie thought she was annoyed, but she was overcome. The quick straightforward compliment had been as genuine and as little thought-out as Lesley's dreadful—"I simply can't stand the sight of you," and the relief of it was so big that she was afraid she might show too much pleasure. To hide her embarrassment she tried a tragic gesture.

"Well, you're the only person who will," she said darkly.

"Don't be silly, Susan. Why, you know——"

"Yes. I know, and you don't. And you won't, and that's all there is to say about it."

Binkie did not press for further information, but she knew now that Susan wasn't angry with or tired of her, and that was a relief. She must watch and try to find out what was on her mind, and make things right for her. In books, people had splendid chances to prove friendship. They saved one another's lives, bore false accusations with set white faces, performed wonderful acts of secret self-sacrifice. Binkie could not see herself doing any heroic act for Susan—Susan was so complete, so independent. Besides, she would probably think it very silly. She laughed at nearly everything—except when she was in a mood like her present one, the worst of the kind she had ever had.

Perhaps she was disappointed about the ineligibility of the IIIB garden for the prize. That would be top in her mind just now, for the school garden party was to take place in a week— and the shield would be awarded then. That must be it. If there were only a way to make her forget that disappointment and that horrid episode with Rose which Binkie could not bear to think of, as it made her heart tighten with a sort of shame. There must be some possibility—the form-garden competition could not be the only interesting event on that day.

Nothing, however, suggested itself. On the night before the

garden party Binkie wandered about alone, wishing that she hadn't done her lessons, wishing that she had enough energy to play a three with Mona and Lilian, wishing that someone else were as good as Susan, who, with the mouth-organ and a book from the school library, had gone off by herself. She had a curious habit of reading and playing the tuneless tune at the same time— but Binkie had not heard the tune for nearly three weeks now. Certainly there was something very wrong with Susan.

"Hullo, Binks! I've been looking for you all over the place."

"*Rose!*" Binkie flung her arms round her sister and gave her a hard hug. It was so good to see Rose, beautiful and certain, rather weary-eyed, but fresh in her clean white linen tennis things, and smelling of bath salts, and a bit of mignonette she wore stuck in her belt.

"Anything wrong?" Rose disengaged herself from Binkie's embrace, and took her arm to walk her towards school. Her voice was a little concerned—the rapturous welcome suggested reaction from loneliness.

"Oh no. Only I'm so glad to see you back. Were the papers terrible? Do you think you'll get a schol.?"

"They weren't particularly terrible, but I didn't do them particularly well," said Rose. "I couldn't sleep properly: my brain got so clever in the night. However, it's useless to talk about them now. We'll know quite soon."

"Show me the papers."

"Rhoda and Lel have them. There they are. But *you* won't be interested in them, Binkie."

"Oh, *do* let me see them."

Rose looked amused, and, taking the bundle of papers from Lesley, gave it to Binkie, who at once began to study questions on Latin and Greek with an air of rapturous reverence combined with old experience in such things.

"My word, what a week you must have had!" exclaimed Rhoda.

"And, Rose, I don't know what you'll say to us. Do you know

"Hullo, Binks!"

"Hullo, Piglet"

what we have just remembered that we have forgotten to do?"

Rose didn't.

"Order flowers to decorate the lunch-room to-morrow."

"Well, we can phone down to the nurseries now, can't we?"

"They don't take orders after six. It's now half-past seven."

"Get them first thing to-morrow."

"But it's a long way to go, and Edmund Ironsides insists that everything shall be ready by eleven."

"Well, surely there's plenty of stuff in the garden."

"That's the difficulty. The form gardens are the best part of the garden, and naturally the forms won't want to pick their showiest flowers just before the prize is awarded."

"What about the roses on the terrace?"

"The terrace roses aren't the decorative kind. They're past their best, too—they still look all right in masses, but they won't look so nice in Edmund Ironsides' room. And she likes the thing well done, you know."

"It's a pity, that," said Rose.

"It's more than a pity. I'm awfully sorry, Rose. We ought to have remembered. You look after everything so well while you're here, and we're as helpless as infants when we're left to ourselves."

"Oh, rubbish," said Rose, but she knit her brows. It was a pity. School patrons and important visitors lunched with Miss Edmund in her own room, and it had for many years been the pride of the Sixth to decorate it for the occasion. Sometimes they would delegate the arrangement of the flowers to some particularly talented Fifth Former, but they, and they alone, were responsible for seeing that the thing was done.

"*Flowers!*" cried Binkie, suddenly looking up from her fascinated contemplation of a Greek unseen. "Oh, we can give you flowers. Heaps of them."

"You?"

"Yes. IIIB."

"But the shield?"

"Don't you remember? We're out of the Shield Competition."

Rose flushed a little.

"For that very reason IIIB mayn't be particularly anxious to give their flowers."

"Oh, they will! I know they will. Besides, it's only Susan and me, really. We've grown the flowers. And Miss Loraine. Miss Loraine won't mind."

Rose took hold of Binkie by the shirt collar and gave her a little friendly shake.

"Learn, my child, not to speak for the mob until you have consulted it, otherwise you may be torn limb from limb."

"But I am the mob," said Binkie. "*I'm* IIIB."

The other girls laughed.

"There's something in the idea," said Rhoda. "They have some beautiful stuff in their garden. I was admiring it from a safe distance the other day. Mind, Binkie, it's the big things, the irises, for instance, we want. No good rooting up lobelias and calceolarias."

"I know. And we have some sweet peas, already—just a few in the hot corner. I'm so glad. I'll go and tell Susan."

"Look here," said Lesley, "I don't think this plan any good at all."

"Why on earth not?" inquired Rhoda. "If these people like to give their stuff, why shouldn't they? Very good of them, I think—and very good stuff, too."

"It isn't that," said Lesley uncomfortably. "It's—"

"Oh, Lel, don't," said Rhoda. "Cut away, Binkie, and see the others. It's a splendid idea."

Binkie looked at Rose.

"See what they say, anyhow," granted Rose.

Binkie flew off. She was so glad that IIIB were to use their flowers for a lofty purpose that she did not reflect upon the doubtful demeanour of Lesley and Rose. It would be proud and glorious to go down to the garden, choose a beautiful colour scheme, gather the flowers, and present them. Perhaps the Sixth would allow Susan and herself to help to arrange them. IIIB would not be out of it after all. Susan would be so glad. Binkie skipped as she ran—anticipating the pleasure of seeing Susan come right out of that mood, and be funny and gay as she used to be.

She found Susan huddled up on the other side of the little stream in the field, now almost concealed by rushes. She wasn't reading, but watching—probably for reed-warblers or water-rats. But Binkie, though generally considerate of the feelings of a naturalist, was in no mood to remember the advisability of stealth and noiselessness in approach. She crashed through the rushes, jumped the summer-shrunken brook, and flung herself down by Susan's side.

"Oh, Susan!"

"What's the matter? Oh, Binkie—he's gone!"

"Who?"

"That little bird. He was a sedge-warbler, I think. He had white eyebrows—I could see them quite plainly. He was so near. Well, it's no good now. What's the matter?"

Somewhat damped, but still certain of Susan's enthusiasm, Binkie told her. Susan drew up her knees to her chin, and listened attentively, but didn't say a word.

"Aren't you glad?" finished Binkie. "Do say you are glad, Susan. It's so nice to be in it."

"We shouldn't have been in it if the Sixth hadn't forgotten to give their order," said Susan.

"Oh, but still, we needn't bother about that, need we?"

"We shall have to cut all those irises," said Susan.

Binkie said nothing; she felt too horribly disappointed. She did not know the real gardener's instinct, which Susan had, the delight in gloating over a lovely thing grown, the tug of giving it up, seeing it go into a room, seeing the clump of green leaves left without it, like a throne without a beautiful queen; and she knew nothing of the anger in Susan because of Lesley and Rose. She sat quite still, looking at the reeds where Susan must have seen the warbler, all the joyful excitement blotted out of her face. But she wasn't going to show Susan that she minded, and she didn't intend to persuade or blame her. Susan sat very still too, staring straight in front of her. Then she put her hand on Binkie's knee.

"All right, Binks," she said. "Let's have a look at the garden, and see what we'll give."

"Do you want to, Susan? Sure?"

"Yes, of course. Of course I'm glad. Imagine growing flowers for the table of Edmund Ironsides, Binks! We'll get a commission from Jupiter and Juno next. IIIB, forsooth! Come along—let's choose the ones we'll cut."

She spoke with a great show of enthusiasm, and Binkie saw that she was doing her very best. So she resolutely cheered up too.

"We had better see Miss Loraine first, and tell IIIB."

"IIIB? What have they got to do with it?"

"Well, it's their garden, Susan."

"You surprise me, Binks! I suppose it is. They're Lord and Lady Vere de Vere, and we're the poor blokes wot does the gardening."

"You tell Miss Loraine, and I'll see IIIB," said Binkie, with wisdom beyond her years. "She's probably down at the garden now. Let's hope she hasn't picked all the irises in a fit of absent-mindedness. Talk to her, Susan, till I come back."

Now somewhat daunted, and doubtful of success, Binkie found IIIB scattered around the tennis courts, gathered them together, and told them of the suggestion made to the prefects. She treated the matter with much tact, representing IIIB as the possible saviours of a situation created by the folly and forgetfulness of the Olympian Sixth. This appealed to IIIB, who, like most people, enjoyed the sensation of importance. Almost at once they rose to the occasion.

"It's for the honour of the school!" said Mona Manders, always ready with something she had got out of a book. "Well played, IIIB."

"It's all Binkie," said Lilian. "She has done more work in that garden than all the rest of us put together."

"It's quite true," cried two or three girls. "Cheers for Binkie!"

Binkie looked alarmed, and, in her embarrassment, took off her sailor hat (everyone had been forced to wear a hat in the garden during the month of July since a IIIB had been sick while weeding—this was supposed by authority to be due to the heat of the sun; IIIB attributed it to something far more humiliating), and put it on again back to front. Then she went off to the garden to find Susan.

Susan was there by herself, kneeling on the earth by a clump of irises, firmly smoothing their long sword-like leaves, and touching their lovely flaunting petals so gently that they could have felt her finger-tips no more than the edge of a butterfly's wings.

"How she likes them," thought Binkie, and for a moment saw the garden without them. She went softly up to Susan, wishing she had not been so quick to boast to the Sixth of the IIIB flowers and their willingness to give them. But when Susan turned and began to talk there was not a trace of regret in her face or voice.

"We'll make it lovely, Binks," she said. "Irises in those tall straight jars Edmund Ironsides has, and sweet peas in something clear and light, and very dark pansies, the purple ones that are almost black, on the table. Do you think the Sixth will let us do it ourselves?"

"They'll *want* you to do it," said Binkie, though her evening experience of speaking for other people made her feel a little doubtful inside. "No one else could do it so well. I'll go now—I'll go and tell Rose."

CHAPTER XV

The Mystery Solved

By good luck Binkie found Rose playing tennis with Rhoda, and both the seniors said that Susan might arrange the flowers, and that they would settle with the rest of the Sixth. "She won't mind if we just look at them afterwards, I suppose?" said Rose politely. "We're responsible, you see." And Binkie, believing that Susan would make a success of whatever she chose to do, that she wouldn't care to try things she couldn't do properly, said that Susan would want the Sixth to look at them. But she said nothing about this statement to Susan, who, very quiet and business-like and detached, shut herself up in the little cloak-room with Miss Edmund's jars and a heap of irises and sweet peas and dark pansies for an hour and a half; at the end of which time she summoned Binkie by a blast on the mouth-organ, and the two, tiptoe as if in church, carried the flowers to Miss Edmund's room, and, reverently as if they were votive offerings, arranged them there. When they had finished, they stood for a minute clutching one another's hands and gloating—but only for a minute, as it was nearly eleven, and there was no time for contemplation of what had been done. The usual day followed. The school hooked or buttoned or pulled itself into its white frocks, and tied its black hair-ribbons. There were nice things to eat for tea, and the III's, their mouths watering, loyally saw that the guests were served with them. There was much talk about the garden and certain flower competitions, and Rose got a prize for making a man's buttonhole, a tiny sprig of Sweet William. There was a pastoral play by the Fifth, which none of the smaller girls, behind the guests, as even small hostesses should be, could see or hear very well. IIIA won their shield, and, suddenly noble in triumph, reserved comment on their prowess to IIIB till the next day. A few people spilt tea or ices down their white frocks, and wondered if the stain would come out in the wash, before their mothers saw it. Everyone was very gay, and proud of St. Helen's, either because she was in it, or had had the good sense and taste to send her daughters to it, or knew someone there growing up to be "such a nice girl". Altogether the thing was a success, as Miss Edmund's things generally were, for she set courtesy to guests high, and her girls did the same.

Susan and Binkie had been too busy and curious all day to think much about the IIIB flowers. Both of them were startled when Miss Edmund suddenly swept towards them and addressed them as, a little limp and dishevelled, they were helping to clear away deck-chairs and cups and saucers at the end of the day.

"I was delighted with your flowers, and they are beautiful," she said. "Miss Loraine tells me that you have worked hard in your garden this summer."

"Susan arranged them," said Binkie.

"So I understand," said Miss Edmund. "They were done most delicately, and the colour scheme suited my room admirably. Thank you, Susan."

She was gone, and Susan, with an air of extreme nonchalance, lifted a particularly big chair and carried it off. But she tripped over nothing, and nearly fell down, and Binkie knew she was excited and happy. Miss Edmund's praise did not come often, and was always well deserved.

"That child Susan did those flowers well," said Rose, dropping on to a window-seat in the prefect's study, and nearly upsetting a bowl of Lesley's cherished specimens. "She's a clever child. Artistic temperament, I should think."

"Yes," growled Lesley. "That is exactly what I should think too."

"You haven't a shred of respect for Susan, Lel," said Rose. "Have you?"

"Well, I don't know about that." As often happens, Lesley's statement of extreme dislike to poor Susan herself had been followed by a reaction, and she once or twice wished she had not said it, wondered if it were true. "But I can't understand you, Rose. Honestly, I think you're a bit sentimental about that young sister of yours."

"Me? Sentimental? Binks? Rubbish!" remarked Rose tersely.

"But look at the thing straight, Rose. Are you all your life going to stand anything from anybody just because your sister is interested in him or her?"

"Certainly not."

"Well—" Lesley's expression and gesture were eloquent.

"I know you think I'm wrong about Susan. But I'm not sure—I know she was rather cheeky to me months ago, before Binks swam upon the horizon, but you can't go on nourishing old grievances for ever."

"For ever! Old grievances!"

"Well—perhaps we were a bit drastic about that mouth-organ. I almost think the child was just blasting away on it without reflecting on the nuisance she was to us. It's a common complaint, Lel. If you lived in a flat in London you'd know that music is like a motor-cycle—you don't notice the row when you're responsible for it yourself."

Lesley snorted.

"That affair was chiefly mine, anyway. But your chart—and those unspeakable pickle-bottles."

Rose suddenly sat up.

"Lel, we don't *know* about that!"

"We do! I do! I had a talk with Susan on the subject. She came back up here to put back the mouth-organ, and we had a little conversation—short, sharp, and to the point."

Rose's face changed.

"Oh! And did she say she had done it?"

"Of course she had done it! It was obvious. She was a little dismayed when we cut IIIв out of the junior entertainments, and came across to try and put things right."

"Did she say she had done it?"

"I don't know whether she actually said so—it isn't the sort of thing one would push to proclaim. But she apologized."

Rose leaned out of the window.

"Binkie!" she shouted.

Binkie went on carrying chairs; Myra and Cecil immediately sprang across a flower-bed and stood looking expectantly up at Rose.

"Tell Binkie I want her, please. And—ask Susan Crashaw to come up too, will you?"

The devoted pair fled to do Rose's bidding, and Lesley got up as if to go.

"Oh, stay, Lel. *Do* stay. I'm going to clear up this business, once and for all. That's why I want Binkie. Susan will be too thorny for truth if we have her alone."

Lesley sat down on a low stool in the corner, clasping and unclasping her hands, and staring dismally into a large glass bowl containing a number of small glossy frogs. Rose settled herself on the window-sill, cool and authoritative, but rather sweet. The fight was going out of her, thought Lesley. Perhaps this was due to sentiment, perhaps to brain-fag—anyway it was a pity.

"Come in!" said Rose in answer to Binkie's knock, and in came two small girls in limp white frocks, cheeks flushed and eyes bright with exertion.

"You look hot. Sit down," said Rose. "Thank you, Susan, for arranging the flowers. They are lovely flowers, and done so nicely."

Susan made the usual inarticulate murmur about that being all right, and then there was a short silence, during which Rose wondered why she had been so eager for Lesley to stay. It was

Binkie, surprisingly, who launched the conversation right into the middle of where her sister wanted it to go.

"Rose, have you finished your chart? Do show Susan your chart!" she cried.

"I'll have to do another," said Rose. "My chart is spoilt."

"Spoilt! Oh, Rose, *when*? Did you spill ink on it?"

Lesley stared hard at Susan, who, wonderfully softened, was regarding Rose and Binkie with polite interest.

"No. Somebody sent me a birthday present for a practical joke—two bottles of chutney, piccalilli, something of the sort. Smashed them in through the window on the chart, with love and best wishes, and blue ribbon, and red and white roses—a fearful mess, of course. I didn't think the joke a good one—but I never do think practical jokes very funny, even when they're not played on me."

"Oh, Rose!"

Binkie was staring at Rose with eyes as round as those of the dog the little soldier saw sitting on the money-chest.

"Pretty mean, wasn't it?" cut in Lesley from her corner. "But Rose won't prosecute. I should think that fact will make the person who did it feel rather worse than if she had had a good sharp punishment."

"It won't," said Binkie, "because she doesn't know. *They* don't know."

"What do you mean?" inquired Lesley.

"Oh, poor things!" cried Binkie. "They—oh, I don't know what they'll do."

"Poor Rose, I should say," commented Lesley, still looking intently at Susan, who showed no sign of self-consciousness, merely the rather pained interest the situation seemed to demand.

"What do you mean, Binks?" asked Rose. "What do you know about it?"

"Oh, Rose, it's partly my fault. I never guessed it would turn out like this. It's Myra and Cecil—oh, don't be too angry with them; they'll languish away and die, or do something desperate if you are. You see, they wanted to give you a birthday present, and were saving up, and thought of chocolates from Buszard's. They said to me—'What does Rose like to eat?' and I said: 'Pickles.' You do, you know, Rose, don't you? You know you always say you would put on a menu Horse Radish and Beef, or Mint Sauce and Mutton, or Chutney and Cold Pork—the most important thing first instead of second. They were rather disappointed, because they thought it an unromantic sort of present to give you, and they asked me two or three times if it were really true, and I said yes, it really was. So Myra sneaked into Miller & Hill's one day when Mam'selle was taking the walk, and got two bottles. They washed the bottles with hot water and sandalwood soap to make them shinier, and Cecil took the blue ribbon out of her best night-gown to tie on the birthday greetings, and they stuck roses in the ribbon to make it look more like the kind of present they thought you ought to have. And they asked me to give them to you, and I said no, they had better do it themselves, because I had just been giving you the Euripides, and I know you don't like me to buzz round the prefects' study. They got very nervous, so I said: why not drop them in at the window on the little table when you weren't there. Oh, Rose, I thought you had rolled up your chart and put it away."

Binkie stopped, panting for breath. Lesley stared at Susan with an expression as blank as that of one of her own fish. Rose flung back her head and laughed.

"Oh, *Binkie!*" she said. "What an ass you are!"

"Oh, Rose, I know I am."

Binkie looked dejected.

"They saw you wearing the roses," she went on; "and they were beside themselves. They said: 'Ha, ha, 's'all right. She's got them. She's pleased.'"

Everyone laughed this time, even Lesley.

"Didn't they guess that the jars had broken?" she inquired.

"No. They were a bit doubtful at first, because they cracked one when they washed it in hot water, and it was a longer drop from the window than they had thought. But when Rose came down to supper, they thought it must be all right—because of their precious 'Liberty' and 'Bride' they had been watching for days and praying to come out in time."

"Did you notice the mess when you came in to fetch your mouth-organ, Susan?" asked Lesley.

"No. I was in rather a hurry. I knew just where it was, and bolted across to the drawer to get it, and out as quickly as I could."

"That's all right, Lel. Leave that," said Rose.

"No, we can't leave it for a second," said Lesley. "Susan, I must apologize to you. I thought you had sent those pickle bottles to Rose as a practical joke, and smashed them up over her chart. It seemed impossible for anyone to send them in earnest. That made me so angry when you came over with your mouth-organ. I'm sorry."

Susan stared at Lesley.

"But I wouldn't have spoiled Rose's chart," she said.

"I know," broke in Rose. "We misjudged you, both of us. You mustn't be too hard on us, Susan. The whole thing was so queer, and the circumstantial evidence so strong."

"You said yourself it wasn't strong enough," snapped Lesley. "You wouldn't take measures for that reason. No, it's my fault, this affair. If Susan likes to start a deadly feud, it'll have to be with me. If not—have an apple, Susan."

Susan took an apple, a large one, but was rather too much overcome to bite into it. Binkie put her arm round her waist.

"Poor old Susan!" she said. Evidently there was some mystery connected with the mouth-organ, which must be cleared up later, but she knew enough to understand Susan's moodiness during the last few weeks.

"We won't say anything to Myra and Cecil," decided Rose. "You might drop them a hint when they choose their present for the next head girl next year, Binks. But we'll let this affair rest."

"A secret?" said Binkie. "As secret as the Hound of the Baskervilles?"

"Oh, Binks, you baby. I thought you had dropped that hound. As secret as any old thing you like, until I'm out of this school."

A loud cheerful crunching sound indicated that Susan had recovered her spirits sufficiently to take a large bite out of her apple. Binkie felt much cheered. Lesley looked relieved, and Rose set her mouth in the line that keeps back a laugh.

"You had better go now," she said. "Time for supper, if not bed. But we'll see you again soon—and the rest of IIIB. Good-night, Susan."

"Good-night, Rose."

They gave one another a quick look, and Binkie hugged herself as she went off with Susan.

"It's all right," she told herself. "Susan and Rose like one another now. *Really* like one another. It's all right. Hurrah!"

CHAPTER XVI

A Swimming Match

It was hot.

Outside, the wasps hung on the red and purple fuchsias, and the heat lay in a grey haze over the garden. If you put your hand on the gravel of the path it felt like the top of a stove; even the long grass was warm. The sun, pouring through the glass roof of the swimming-baths, smote down on the green water, which generally made you shiver, but which was tepid this afternoon. In spite of the heat, every bench in the gallery was crowded. Girls who had been too busy with examinations or had not enough skill to enter for the sports, mistresses, day-girls and their people, sat watching with interest and amusement, fanning themselves with straw hats or linen hats or programmes of events, saying at intervals how hot it was and how they wished they were in the water, sighing for ices and gratefully drinking the lemonade which Miss Watkins, the cook, made in buckets for days like this, and which non-competitors in Forms III carried round in long thin tumblers with straws. But at four o'clock Forms III put down their trays and stood in the back row of the gallery, straining as far forward as they could without endangering the existence of those in front, and no one expected anything else of them. For at ten minutes past four came the great event of the afternoon—the final for the form shield, to be swum by IIIA and IIIB.

The fact that IIIB had survived to swim the final Binkie attributed to sheer good luck. It had drawn with Form V, a rather weak lot, bound to be knocked out in the first heat. Then it had swum the Lower Fourth, and the Lower Fourth had incurred a penalty for a false start, from which it had been unable to recover.

It was ridiculous, of course, but it was great. Binkie leaned against the hot brick wall, pulling down her cap over her eyes, a thin little resolute figure in the scanty gaily-striped costume that reached from somewhere below her neck to somewhere above her knees. Mona, important and confident, sat on the ground beside her. There was one thing about Mona—you could count on her to do all she could. There was not a nerve in her constitution; she never surpassed herself, but never fell short of her powers. Looking down at her broad back, Binkie felt a sudden respect and affection for old Mona. It was rather wonderful, the way she had patiently learned to swim, and was actually taking part in a match—was actually in the IIIb team. The IIIb team! Binkie grinned to herself, looking up in the gallery for the rest of the form. She could not see them; they were too far back; but she saw Miss Loraine, her elbows on the rail, her chin propped on her hand in an attitude of intense interest, or intense gloom— Binkie did not know which. Rose and Lesley were sitting by her. They smiled and made friendly signs, and Binkie straightened herself, and folded her arms so that their small muscles bulged out, as she knew swimming champions did when photographed. She was excited, and a little nerve was beating uncomfortably in her forehead, but it was fun to swim in the form final, and, even though IIIb must be beaten, she meant to put up a good fight and enjoy it.

"Binkie!" Susan pattered up and stood by her. Binkie had reserved her strength for this race, but Susan had been in for nearly everything. During the obstacle race she had struggled in a tub for so long that Binkie had thought she must perish in it, and she had lost a little three-cornered bit of flesh from the bridge of her nose in a water-polo match. She said that these episodes heartened her; that if she were to stand on the brink of the bath all the afternoon she would be unwilling to move a limb when desired to do so. But Binkie, gravely surveying her, thought she had, as usual, wasted her energy.

"You're to swim last. Miss Loraine says you're the one to save the situation, if there is one."

Binkie felt the top of her cap with a comical look.

"You're faster than I am, Susan."

"I know. That's not the point, Miss Loraine says. Mona, don't start before the whistle, as that incomparable ass in Lower Four did."

"Trust Mona," said Binkie, giving Mona's back a little nudge with her bare foot. "Mona's all right."

"Get in, Mona, and hang on. IIIA's in."

Deliberately Mona lowered herself in, and hung on to the chain, surveying the scene with a Napoleonic air of resolution. Susan ran off to the opposite end, to be ready when Mona touched, and Binkie sat down on the edge of the bath, dipping her toes into the water. Cecil was sitting by her. Cecil was a renowned prize-winner. Mysterious letters and badges crowded along the yoke of her swimming-dress. She did not look at all excited. In fact, she seemed a little bored. It must be rather boring for a team like IIIA to swim IIIB. Binkie's chin got rather squarer, and Rose, watching her from the gallery, laughed.

"Ready—Form Shield Final!"

Miss Lucas's big voice and shrill whistle. A scuffle and murmur from the crowded benches. Binkie suddenly saw nothing in the world but the face of Susan, as she hung from the opposite chain, one foot against the tiled side to give herself a good shove-off, one arm stretched out ready for her stroke. She knew that Mona, just below her, was in the same attitude, but what Mona did didn't matter much. What Susan did mattered a great deal.

"One—two—three—away!"

Binkie shut her eyes a moment, and her heart began to pound. Then she opened them, and slipped right into the water to steady her excitement by the shock. Shouts came from the gallery.

"Go on, IIIA! Go on! Oh, good! Cheers for IIIA!"

What need to cheer IIIA, she wondered. She had known IIIB

was in a bad case, but she had not known it was as bad as this. It was pitiful to see Mona patiently and slowly swimming her beginner's breast-stroke, while Myra, with a long smooth lovely side-stroke, slipped away past her, and reached the opposite end before she had done more than half the distance.

"Touched—IIIA!"

The second IIIA girl plunged off. Binkie at once saw that she was not so easy a swimmer as Myra. So IIIA's tactics were to swim their weakest second—and suddenly Binkie thought that this was right. Susan could never make up what Mona had lost— never, at her very best, and she must be tired after her varied performances that afternoon.

"Touched—IIIB!"

A loyal roar from the back of the gallery, and Susan dashed from her chain. Binkie felt a shiver of excitement. Supposing, when her turn came, she couldn't move? Supposing, in her anxiety, she made a false start? Supposing—

"Oh, be quiet, and attend," she said to herself, and stared at Susan's face, Susan's white straining face, coming towards her in a great splashing wave. Was Susan right? Did her noisy swimming flummox her opponent? Certainly, she sounded nearer to the IIIA girl than she was. ... But she was rather near. It was coming on, that white face, that white straining face. Oh, Susan was doing splendidly! She mustn't fail her at the end, she simply mustn't.

"Touched—IIIA!"

A huge shout of exultation. Cecil was off.

"Oh, come on, Susan," prayed Binkie in her heart. "Don't listen to that! Don't notice it! Come on! Come on!"

"*Touched*—IIIB!"

She had started. She was swimming. No one had called her back; she was right. She could see Cecil's striped side, just in front of her. Come on! Try that thrusting stroke—it makes you a bit tired, but you can do it, do it well. Cecil has pace—so have you. Come on! You can catch her, overtake her. Thrust on through that great mass of wavy, pushing water—you're getting through—making up on her—getting through.

Somewhere, far, far away, came great shouts and cries and roars.

"Go on, IIIB! Played! Come on—come on—you've got her! Binkie—Binks—Bink-ee-ee. Oh, *good!* Good man! Don't stop! Go on! Well played! Binkie! Oh—played—*played*—PLAYED— Ah-h-h-h!"

Then a little thin whistle, surprisingly near, and a strangely calm voice—

"Touched—IIIB."

Binkie clambered up on the chain, and, dead beat, fell back again into the water. Miss Lucas seized her arm and hauled her out, and she sat on the side, too limp to scramble to her feet, but with something like a flame shooting up inside her. She saw Cecil, standing by her, and panting, give her a quick little smile before she walked off to her box—the smile with which St. Helen's acknowledged defeat. And she heard a hurricane of voices.

"IIIB! Well played! Three cheers! Three cheers for Binkie! Binkie of IIIB!"

Then Rose was beside her.

"For goodness sake, child, hustle off to your box and get that bathing-cap off before it bursts. Come along. Hurry up. Tea is ready for IIIB."

Rose was tremendously pleased. Binkie obediently struggled to her feet, pulled off her bathing-cap, and pattered off to her box, suddenly shy as the shouts were renewed.

"Binkie Seymour?" "Rose Seymour's sister." "The head girl's sister?" "Rose—the girl who won the scholarship?" "Surely she'll distinguish herself too?" "Oh yes, a good little tadpole." "In IIIB?" "But IIIB was such a dud form." "Well, it's not now. Nothing stays dud with a Seymour in it." "And that child Susan swam well." "And their garden." "Miss Edmund's flowers." "Susan did those." "Susan and Binkie." "Binkie Seymour." "Binkie of IIIB."

Such were the scraps that might have been gleaned by the interested as IIIB surged out of the building. Rose got some of them; so did Lesley; so did Miss Loraine; so, with modestly averted eyes and ears which mercifully did not appear pricked up, did Susan and Binkie.

"Rose said: 'Tea is ready for IIIB,'" said Binkie to Susan, as, towels and swimming-dresses rolled into tight wet sausages and stowed under their arms, they left the baths. "I don't know what she meant by that."

"Come and see." Lesley, walking in front with a group of palpitating and flushed and dishevelled IIIB's, turned with a friendly smile. And Binkie gave a little skip, taking Susan's arm. Evidently something really satisfactory was going to happen.

It was. Under the lime trees in the garden a long table was set out, decorated with cornflowers and marigolds, a scheme which Susan eyed critically, but which she approved when she remembered that the school colours were orange and blue. And on the table were all the things third-formers like to eat: buns with currants, buns with sultanas, buns with candied peel, cakes with icing, cakes with frills, squashy-middles oozing cream, gooseberries and raspberries and nougat. At the head of the table sat Miss Loraine, looking entirely lost but quite happy, and someone had given her a large button-hole of cornflowers and marigolds, which dangled dangerously from her tie-pin. Binkie and Susan, without a word to anyone, immediately sat down, one on either side of her. Opposite her, at the end of the table, was propped up the shield, blazoned on which a little mermaid clasped hands with a little girl in the St. Helen's swimming stripes. And the Sixth carried round cups of tea, with the politest conversation, while IIIB, overcome, said: "Oh yes. No, *really*. Thank you. One lump, please. Yes, that's very nice. Oh, *don't* bother. Oh, *thank* you."

"Won't the shield look nice hanging up in the form-room, Miss Loraine?" inquired Susan. Whereupon a satisfied gulp caused Binkie to look sharply to her right, and witness Mona Manders recovering from an incipient choking fit caused by the surge of pride in ownership.

"I think I must come in during the holidays to look at it," said Miss Loraine, gazing dreamily at it. "I did not think I should ever have a form which won a shield."

"Ha, ha!" said IIIB. "You see!"

"We shall all be moved up next year, so you'll have it all to yourself, Miss Loraine," said Susan, with a twinkle.

Miss Loraine looked vaguely alarmed.

"Oh, of course," she said. "So you will. You'll be in IVA, Binkie."

Binkie did not look as pleased as she would have done at the beginning of the term.

"If it's not asking too much, Miss Loraine, would you mind telling me where Susan is to be?" she asked, with all the politeness and tact learned from Rose.

"Susan! Oh, Susan is to go to IVA too. Miss Edmund thinks that Susan has done well this term."

"Does it say so on my report?" inquired Susan suspiciously.

But Miss Loraine would give away no more state secrets. She looked at Susan for a minute, and then gave her that excellent and world-famous piece of advice—to wait and see.

"I shan't like IVA nearly as well as IIIB," said Binkie with sudden conviction.

"But you hated being in IIIB at the beginning," said Susan.

"That was my fault, I believe," said Rose, pouring out more tea for Miss Loraine. "But Binkie had rather more sense than I, which was a good thing. However, you *will* like IVA, Binks. Wait and see."

"I shall be so old in IVA," said Binkie. "Thirteen. I shall be called Elizabeth then."

"Elizabeth Seymour is a good name," said Miss Loraine.

"I know. Binkie is silly—Mother hates it. But people call

babies by those names, and then they can't get out of it when the babies grow up."

"I believe I'll always think of you as Binkie," said Susan. "Even when you're an old lady with a little bag and a fat dog."

"So shall I," said Miss Loraine. "Binkie of IIIв."

Binkie chuckled. She wasn't any longer just Rose Seymour's sister, or even Binkie Seymour, but Binkie of IIIв.

Funny to feel proud of a title like that.

But she did.

BLACKIE'S REPRINT
(UNDATED)

With frontispice by Louis Ward

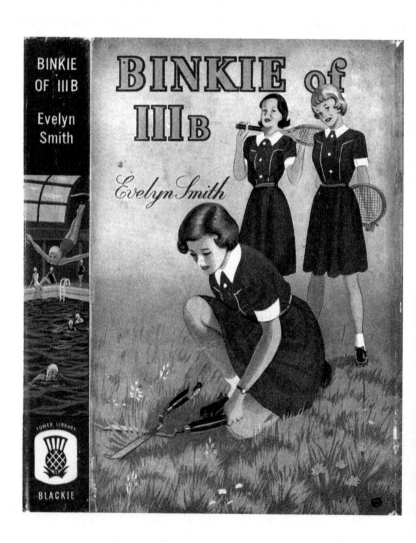

Discipline is maintained

The Inkpot Lid

A School Story By
Evelyn Smith

BECKY BURKE!"
Becky Burke stood up, not very quickly, but quickly
enough to surprise herself into upsetting a pencil-box which had
been so precariously placed on the edge of her desk that a more
ethereal creature than a small girl of nine would not have been
able to move without overturning it. The class smiled and sighed.
Becky Burke was so well known to be incapable of changing her
position without a crash, that the fact had almost ceased to be
funny. To Miss Mortlake, who was responsible for the instruction
and manners of Form Lower Three, and whose nervous system
was not of the best, it had never been anything but irritating.
Her eyebrows now drew themselves together in a way that Becky
hated, because it meant that she was too much harassed to scold.
If you were irritating and a mistress made a sarcastic remark, the
two things cancelled, and need not be counted any more. But a
look like that was inexplicable—the thought of what might be
rankling in Miss Mortlake's mind for ever was terrifying. Becky
blinked, said, "Oh, dear!" and stared at the scattered contents of
the box as if they had suddenly dropped from realms above and
she had never before set eyes on them.

"You need not pick them up now," said the mistress wearily.
"The end of the period will do, as you are to move your desk
in any case. As Mrs. Thursby quite reasonably objects to Pearl
coming home covered with ink, you had better sit by yourself—
in the single desk at the back of the room."

Becky, who was a sociable being, gave a little gasp and turned
to look at the single desk at the back of the room, though she

knew its appearance quite well. It was the only one of its kind, and the idea of being marooned, as it were, on a small island by oneself, while everyone else enjoyed life with a friend at a double desk, was insupportable. She turned mournful grey eyes upon Miss Mortlake, but the mistress was glancing over a letter which she held in one hand, and did not look at her. Slowly she sank into her seat again and opened her French book. At once a penwiper rolled to the ground. Fortunately, it was made of soft black velvet in the shape of a cat, and its fall was noiseless. She remembered now that she had put him in the middle of a story about *une souris,* because she felt he would enjoy it so. She made a dive and recaptured him, but she did not bother to put him back between those particular appetising pages. She wasn't happy herself, and she didn't care about the feelings of her possessions.

Remorsefully she looked at Pearl Thursby, who shared her present double desk, and, this morning, would not look at her. She admired Pearl, who was pretty and neat, with shining, fair hair and blue or pink frocks that never had a tear or stain, unless someone else's carelessness blemished them. It had really been rather awful yesterday when the whole inkpot leapt from its socket on the point of Becky's pen and a great blot shaped like Australia immediately formed on Pearl's pink sleeve. Pearl had cried a little. She was afraid of what her mother would say, as the pink dress was new. Someone had suggested milk, and Becky had eagerly bought a glass at lunch and poured it over the sleeve; but the blot had merely elongated itself to the south-east, and now looked like South Africa instead of Australia. Pearl's mother must have been very angry to have written to Miss Mortlake. Becky tried to imagine her own mother writing to the form mistress when, say, Rosalind Pierce had pulled the green glass eyes out of the cat penwiper. That had been frightfully annoying, but Mrs. Burke didn't seem to think that it mattered much. For an instant Becky felt aggrieved—not longer, for she had a way of accepting her misfortunes as her own fault, which, indeed, they generally were. She knew herself smudgy and untidy and clumsy; people at home and in school were always saying so. Opinion so general must be right.

At the end of the morning she was left alone to move her books into her new place, probably because Miss Mortlake's nerves would not have stood the strain of listening to the process. There were many bumps and bangs before her possessions were pushed in, and she found that the lid would just shut. It was as she was leaning on it to make certain that it really came down properly over the chaos within that she realized certain qualities about her new desk.

It was varnished brown, like all the rest, but whereas they were hacked and chipped and blotted, its surface was quite glossy and smooth. That did not appeal to Becky—she liked tracing initials carved by people who were now in the Fifth and Sixth, and fitting her pencil-points into small deep burrows made by those of her predecessors. But there was something else. Each of the other desks had simply a small hole to accommodate a dull, chipped china inkpot, but hers had a hole with a lid—a bright lid, undulled and unblotted, shining on the right of her desk like a big gold coin.

She could hardly believe that she was to enjoy such distinction. Miss Mortlake couldn't have noticed. Of course, the desk was new, and no one would have chosen to occupy it because it was single. But that glittering disc that covered the inkwell—always a source of misfortune to Becky—was worth the society of Pearl Thursby, especially since the letter about the blot. It would be a pity if Miss Mortlake were to come quietly in that half-holiday afternoon and see for the first time what a splendid inkpot lid it was, and think it far too good for a girl she had looked at in that mysterious, frowning way. Better conceal it, and make possession safe. Becky flung back the lid of the new desk, and, after a short, crashing rummage, drew out the black cat penwiper, and planted him straight and sure on the shining lid. He just concealed it. His stiff tail lay out along the groove for pens, and Becky drove a drawing-pin through it into the new, varnished wood, so that no one should dust him from his post. Then, with quite a light heart, she went home.

II

"That's really a neat copy, Becky; I can give you eight for that. If you hadn't twiggled that z's tail in such a silly way you might have had ten," said Miss Mortlake.

Becky flushed. The copy was neat—quite the cleanest she had ever done. And her neighbours were so anxious to see the twiggle in the z's tail, straining half out of their desks in order to satisfy their curiosity, that she felt fame to be worth the sacrifice of two marks. Proudly she looked about her, wiping her pen in the woolly inside of the black velvet cat.

"Solitude suits you, I think," went on Miss Mortlake. "I have noticed the improvement in your work for some days—and you are not half so careless as you were. Now, don't celebrate the compliment by dropping something. If you have finished your work, hands in your lap till the other girls are marked."

Becky caught her pen just in time, and looked out of the corner of her eye to see if Miss Mortlake were being nasty. She wasn't; she was being rather nice. Becky gave a wriggle of satisfaction, and, having quickly shut her inkpot, settled down quietly with folded hands, according to instructions, staring at the still unblotted brightness of the wonderful lid.

Wonderful it was. It was her lucky lid, her mascot, though nobody knew about it. It had been given her by the genius of the schoolroom, a fresh, kind spirit who smelt of new books and lived in the stationery cupboard, with a neck whiter than the whitest chalk, lips like red sealing-wax, and, if she once liked you, a heart that stuck to you faster than the gum of report envelopes. As long as it was kept clean and shining the surly, blotted gnome, who had heretofore haunted Becky's books, would be powerless. So she told herself, amusing herself with make-up, sitting so quietly during spare moments like the present that Miss Mortlake marvelled at the extraordinary reformation of a restless, small girl.

The curious thing was that a change had taken place. Becky was so certain of the luck of the lid that she became able to do things she couldn't do before. She tidied her desk because its welter didn't match the shining neatness of her mascot. She was careful not to drop things, because the crash might cause ink to start out and mar its beauty. She would have cared more for its ruin than for that of Pearl's pink frock—though she had been sorry for that, especially as it had meant the loss of Pearl's friendship. For Pearl wasn't really as nice as her frocks made one think she must be. She didn't like Becky because she had made that blot on her sleeve, and she didn't like to hear Miss Mortlake praise her. She suddenly looked round scornfully, long after the others, to view the twiggle of the z's tail.

By this time Becky's hands were out of her lap, and she was lovingly rubbing the inkpot lid with the black velvet cat. It winked shiningly at her as if it appreciated her kindness, and she smiled. Then she felt someone looking at her, and glanced up to see Pearl's curious and contemptuous eyes. She blushed a little and dropped the cat.

Pearl plunged her pen into her inkpot and shook a blot on the gleaming lid—a satisfactory blot, bang in the middle, big and thick and rayed like a black sun.

Rosalind Pierce, who was looking on with interest, laughed, doubling up. Rosalind always laughed at things like that, and yet you couldn't be deep down angry with her. Long ago Becky had forgiven her for blinding the black cat. But you could be really angry with Pearl, as Becky now discovered.

Furiously she seized her blotting paper and smacked it upon the blot; then, with her disengaged hand, she clutched one of Pearl's pretty fair curls and wrenched it as if to tear it out by the roots. Small wonder that Pearl gave a yelp of surprised agony, and Miss Mortlake wheeled round upon Becky.

"I spoke too soon when I spoke of improvement, I see," she said wearily, and her eyebrows went together in the way Becky hated.

III

Becky simply couldn't believe it.

She opened the inkpot lid and looked at its inside. She shut it and stared at its once bright exterior. She opened it again. She rubbed it with one finger; desperately with blotting-paper; more desperately with the black velvet cat.

Quite useless. It was black all over, smeared with ink which had been allowed to dry on, which would never, never come off. Gone was the smart appearance of her desk; gone was all that curious luck which she thought had come with the lid. She sat down and looked sadly at it, dismayed in a way she would have agreed was silly, if anyone had told her about it, at the loss of its brightness.

Then she felt eyes upon her. Pearl and Rosalind were looking at her; Pearl triumphant, Rosalind roguish. At once she opened her books with an immense show of interest, angry because they had seen she cared.

She imagined Pearl carefully painting the lid, dipping a camel-hair brush into the ink, not spilling a drop on her pretty frock. She was glad she had pulled her hair yesterday; she wished she had pulled it a good bit harder.

"Becky Burke, would you mind repeating what I have just said?" asked Miss Mortlake with great politeness.

Becky stood up and made an attempt: "'Parse and analyse the following sentence,'" she suggested.

It was a pity she tried to guess. Miss Mortlake hadn't been talking about grammar, but an imaginative piece of composition,

to be done then and there in class in half an hour on paper, so that
"best book" writing need not be too much of a consideration.
Becky got to know this along with a few home truths in Miss
Mortlake's very best manner. She sat down with a sense that all
the world was against her.

"And don't be hackneyed," Miss Mortlake warned the class.
"None of the 'Little Violet woke up and found it was all a dream'
endings, thank you."

Becky dabbed her pen angrily into her inkpot. No, indeed!
You didn't wake and find it was all a dream. Your lucky lid was
spoilt, and everyone was cross and hateful, and you couldn't
complain and explain, or you would be thought a silly ass. Things
were real, a great deal too much so.

In big black letters she printed her title—THE INKPOT
LID. Then she began to write.

As she went on her face cleared. It was fun describing the
bright, tidy spirit in the stationery cupboard and the untidy gnome
with dusty hair and grey nails prowling about the classroom to
afflict the unwary. "He could make himself flat and sprawly at
will like a big black blot," she wrote. It was fun describing the girl
whom the spirit was trying to rescue from the gnome, and the
inkpot lid seemed to come bright again as she told of its magic
power. She had not nearly finished when Miss Mortlake snapped
out, "Time's up" and at once seized her paper as if to show that
she wouldn't listen to the plea of "Just one more word; mayn't
I finish this sentence?" which sometimes she would grant quite
pleasantly.

The happy half-hour had passed far too quickly, and there was
not another like it for the rest of the miserable day.

But, if Becky had been in school that afternoon, she would
have seen a sight which would have surprised her out of misery
for a long time.

She would have seen Miss Mortlake, not sharp or weary-
looking, but amused and nice, come into the classroom carrying

a bowl of hot soda and water and soft rags and a tin of polish. She would have seen her sit down at the small desk and scrub and scrape and polish the inkpot lid. And she would have seen the lid get brighter and brighter till it shone more gloriously than it had done in its best days. Then she would have seen Miss Mortlake laugh.

But there was no one there to see except the black velvet cat, and Rosalind Pierce had pulled out his green glass eyes. He sat upright on the desk, blind and silent, and, when Miss Mortlake picked him up and put him on the lid, he sat there obediently, blind and silent still.

IV

"By far the best composition is Becky Burke's," said Miss Mortlake, turning over the pile. "In fact, though it isn't very tidy, and some of the spelling is such as never was on land or sea, I have given it full marks. This exercise, as I told you, was a test of imagination and fancy, not writing and spelling. Becky, will you kindly take your hands from your desk while I read part of your work to the class?"

Becky, who had been feeling light and dancey with happiness since she had come to school that morning and seen a little brass sun gleaming on the right corner of her desk, whipped her hands into her lap—then, with extraordinary speed, raised one to grab the black cat and replace him on the inkpot lid. She hadn't wanted to cover it all the morning till now, the last period, but she didn't want it to be too conspicuous while her story was read. Then she looked at Miss Mortlake out of the corner of one eye to see if she were going to make a remark about disobedience.

She wasn't. She just stared at Becky for a second with her eyebrows drawn together, but in her eyes underneath there was a funny, nice look—one of the nicest looks Becky had ever seen.

Then she began to read THE INKPOT LID.

The Little Lost Street

By Evelyn Smith

I

It was an October evening. The deep blue of town twilight crept among roofs and chimney-stacks: in the paved streets lights shone out, yellow and amethyst and ruby-red and glittering green. The palais de danse and the picture palace began to live up to their names: with their jewelled lamp-lit fronts they seemed palaces indeed. It had been raining a little, and the wet pavements gave back the reflections of coloured light, and the rails of the car-tracks shone as if silver-gilt. The shops and offices were closing: from slits of exits people slipped out into the street, to join the crowd rushing away from work to pleasure—high tea, dancing, the kinema, or just mending stockings or reading the paper by the fire. You could almost feel their relief from the tension of the day.

Katherine felt it, and swung along elated, her hands deep in the pockets of the tweed coat that smelt of the heather of the hills, a country-bred girl who knew all the ways of the town, and walked moor path or paved way with the easy confidence of familiarity, sure of knowing where to go, of never being lost. In the pockets were two sixpences, half a crown, and three pennies. Now and then she would roll a coin round her palm. "Money in both pockets," she thought, "money to spend." She didn't care because it was only three and ninepence all told. Her rent was paid—and for the rest, something would happen. Something always did. And when the evening looked like that it was impossible to be depressed. It would be all wrong, like putting on brogues for a dance, and leaving your silver slippers standing under the dressing table.

For a dance! "I don't suppose *I'll* ever go to a dance again," thought Katherine, "but it can't be helped. You can't have everything." "But have you got *anything*?" said one of her secret selves, the one who likes to be the depressing sort of aunt at the party. "Well, then, what *have* you got?" Katherine blinked and saw the little room with the camp bedstead, the table, the ink bottle and the scarlet pen, the Tate cube-sugar box, the three-legged stool, the scrubbing brush and hunk of yellow soap. She had always said you could scrub your room, however hard up you were. And she stuck to it. And she had twenty pounds in the Post Office Savings Bank. And the Nature Column in the *Evening Herald*—that was regular work, that paid the rent, some of it, anyhow. But no dancing slippers! Did it matter, really? It mattered a bit. Not much—not enough to count.

She dived to the left, for the short cut between one main street and the other which led to the block of two-room or single-apartment flats or studios where she lived, with a collection of widely varying individuals alike in the one respect that they all worked fairly hard and failed to draw sufficient attention to themselves to gain any, or satisfactory, remuneration for what they did. Suddenly she wanted to get home, to get to work, whatever it was. And then she saw that she had cut down the wrong street—well, not the wrong one, for it was parallel to her usual way, but one that she did not know. Narrow and solitary it curved between its tall blocks of offices and warehouses, with wet pavements in which the glittering reflections of the lamps swam like golden starfish, and, high up, the folds of a flag, swinging and then streaming straight in a patch of overhead light, and, higher still, the deep deep blue sky with a few white clouds driven over it. Up sprang Katherine's spirits, sunk for a moment at the contemplation of the great gulf fixed between silver slippers and a scrubbing brush. She caressed her three and ninepence, and swung along as if she were walking to music. This was the loveliest little street—why hadn't she found it before? The flag—what luck to see the flag like that—

"O-o-o-o-o-o!"

A groan. Katherine flushed and slackened her walk. She was frightened at groans—scared stiff. She listened. Silence, except for the impersonal blended squeak and toot and rattle of traffic you hear everywhere in town, as you hear movement of branches and grass in the country. Thank goodness, it must have been a delusion.

There was no one here—nothing—

"Oh—dear me! dear me!"

There it was—a lady-like little person with a bit of fur round her neck, sitting on the kerbstone, rocking herself to and fro, and moaning most miserably—exactly as a cook, who had for a short space of time served Katherine's family at home, used to moan, when, as she explained, she'd "'ad a drop".

If Katherine was afraid of groans, she was very much more afraid of individuals who'd 'ad a drop. She couldn't very well leave this distressed lady in the fur necktie to moan unconsoled—and yet how might she take interference? She might be sentimental and clinging, or violent and abusive. Katherine longed to bolt. Most heartily did she wish she had come down the right street, the safe and populated street, where there were plenty of people who, out of mere curiosity, were not only willing but eager to deal with any sort of situation that might arise, the more unusual the better.

"Oh-h-h-h!" The groan was sinking to a deep bass. Katherine pulled on her hat a bit further, strode to the lamp-post, and, bending down, touched the distressed lady's arm.

"I say, is there anything wrong? Can I help?"

A pinched face turned itself up to the lamplight, and a hand in a split kid glove readjusted a toque trimmed with black velvet and violets.

"Those who leave orange-peel lying in the street ought to be arrested," stated a pardonably querulous voice. "'Ow do they know 'oo they've done for? And much they care."

"Oh—is it *that?*" Katherine was agreeably surprised to find that the lady was in her normal senses, and her relief must have sounded in her voice, for a hurt sniff came from behind a ragged veil that dangled from the toque.

"Yes, it *is* that. That's w'at comes of slipping out for a bit of relish for supper. As if I could afford a sprained ankle. 'Aven't I enough to bear without that?"

"D'you think you can get up? Shall I get an ambulance or something?" Katherine looked vaguely up and down the lonely little street.

"Now, *now*. If you talk like that I'll go off, completely. The ambulance means the 'ospital, and I'm not one to stand the wear and tear of institutions. If you'd give me your arm, I'd contrive to 'obble 'ome—if it meant going on me 'ands and knees."

"What about your parcel?" Katherine glanced about for the bit of supper, well enough acquainted with the difficulties of poverty to know how serious a thing it would be to leave this behind.

"Ow, a cat 'ad that," said a sad voice, as the little lady struggled up and clung to Katherine's arm. "On it like a streak o' lightning, 'e was, from the shadders. ... I never could stand these tabby toms," she added. "Nasty big-'eaded brutes, always on the sneak and the watch, and artful—"

"What a shame!" Katherine was sympathetic enough now. To see one's bit of fish, or whatever it might be, filched before one's very eyes! Carefully she guided the steps of her protégée, who, with a hop and a drag, accompanied with deep sighs and an occasional "ow!" of pain, managed to get herself along the street. And as soon as that heavy, lean little figure was dependent on her, Katherine began to feel quite fond of her, and as eager to see her safely and happily ensconced at home as she would have been to tell one of her own stories to the end.

"Where do you live?"

The little lady stopped, made an attempt to rummage in a once stylish handbag for a card, and gave it up.

"Eighteen, Courtenay Buildings, it is, Miss—Miss—"

"Lovatt. And I live in 16, so I'll see you right home."

"Ow, then you'll know about me. Miss Dupré, theatrical costumière. 'Iring out, mostly, for fancy balls and that sort of thing—I never could abide ordinary dressmaking, but there's a bit of novelty about this."

"Oh yes, I know," said Katherine, wondering if she did, but with a vague memory of a tarnished plate and a parlour window containing a few dusty masks, a powdered wig, and a length of faded art muslin. She wondered at the "Dupré" along with the Midland accent, but there were more surprising things than incongruous names in Courtenay Buildings.

"Look here, I think you'd better have a taxi," she said, as she felt Miss Dupré give a twitch of real pain. And, without waiting for the denial she knew would come, she turned and waved up one apparently hovering in case of need, and got her charge in. One and six—it couldn't be more than one and six—sixpence for a tip—two shillings—one and nine left. She'd see Miss Dupré safely on her sofa and dash out for something else for supper. The tabby tom decamping with the bit of fried fish seemed a misfortune almost equal to the sprained ankle—it was such an insult, somehow.

*

Evidently a "Vera" came in now and then to "do a bit", and, at Miss Dupré's apologetic suggestion, Katherine called on Vera, whom she discovered, her hair in rags, writing a composition on "My Ideal Holiday", to impress the class to-morrow. Vera promised to "pop along" immediately, and, giving her the paper parcel in which was wrapped a bit of cooked meat from the

"I say, is there anything wrong? Can I help?"

Delicatessen at the corner, and a bag containing half a pound of Almeria grapes, Katherine turned towards home. She had sixpence in her pocket—sixpence wasn't much, not as safe a protection as three and ninepence against being really hungry. That little street—had Miss Dupré's distress really sent a sort of wireless signal to her, and compelled her to take the unusual turning? She thought of the small airless room, crammed with faded, stained costumes for masquerade, and battered theatrical properties. She didn't care for the little room—it made her feel as if she must pant for breath—but she rather liked Miss Dupré. She would go again and see her and take her a bunch of violets— she must like violets, as she wore imitation ones in her toque.

Katherine unlocked her door, picked up her letters, went to the window and flung it wide open. The room smelt damp and clean—all right in its way, but better if she could have had a fire burning. She sat down on the Tate cube-sugar box and tore open her letters. One rejected MS.; one dentist's bill—she had forgotten all about that unbearable toothache a couple of months ago; one short note, stiff and annoyed, from an aunt who thought she was mad, and a little wicked too. She leaned her chin on her hand and wondered if this was right. When her mother died, should she have accepted the comfortable home, with the companionship of two cousins (who did nothing but knit jumpers and talk about themselves), and some light housework? There were no books in the house, and there was nothing really hard to do, and never never would she have been alone. No, she couldn't have endured it. It was stuffier than Miss Dupré's little room. But what was to happen to her? She looked at the MS. lying on the table—she had put it down there quite gently, having expected its arrival—and looked at the black grate. She jerked open a box of matches and lighted the fire. She must have a fire on her unlucky evenings— she simply must. Up sprang the flames as if glad to do their best for her—the pity was that they must eat so much wood and coal while doing it. She turned round the sugar box and sat in the firelight, which stained her short, tilted face gold and red, and caught a streak of bronze in her dark hair. She clasped her hands, thin, firm little hands, round her knees, and rocked herself gently backwards and forwards. She wasn't a bit hungry. She wondered what on earth she was going to do. Not to cry, anyhow. Her eyes prickled; a salty lump swelled in her throat. Oh, but she *was*—that was just what she was going to do. In a minute—she really must answer the door first.

II

The ring at the bell was Vera's.

"It's a client," she said breathlessly, "and Miss Dupré's that upset. She'd promised, you see, to get 'im a dominer—'e wouldn't 'ave any in the showroom, being a bit partikeler. She'd meant to look round tonight, an' of course when she'd 'urt 'erself, everything went out of 'er 'ead except 'er sprained ankle."

"But I *haven't* a domino," said Katherine helplessly. "I haven't anything that could pretend to be one, even."

"Miss Dupré'd be so obliged if you'd step round, Miss. 'E don't know what to do, the young feller, because 'is party's to-night, and 'e's got among the stock, and 'e's turning the 'ole place upside down, somethink awful. She thought you might fix up something for him, if only you'd be so kind."

"Right. I'll see what I can do, anyhow," and, slipping on her big coat, Katherine followed the important and distressed Vera, wondering what costume might be evolved from that crushed and faded stock for a young feller as was "a bit partikeler". The demand the episode of the little street had made on her was evidently not yet fulfilled—she'd just see it through to the end.

She found Miss Dupré sitting up on the sofa. Her eyes were bright, and two blotches of red showed on her sallow cheeks. Apparently she took business dealings with proper seriousness, and was thoroughly distressed at the fix of the young man who wanted a fancy dress and couldn't find one to suit him. As for the client himself, he was digging with both hands through a heap of stock, flinging aside togas, and frogged coats, and bits of imitation armour giving at the seams, and garments that seemed of no particular purpose or period.

"There's the Red Cross Knight, Mr. Blakeney," said Miss Dupré tentatively. "It's a great favourite. And it was washed out only last week—the cross has run into the w'ite part a bit, but you'd never notice that from the side."

"The sword's out, Miss Dupré," said Vera in a tragic voice.

"I don't know that you need a sword," said Miss Dupré. "Nasty things, swords are, when you think of it, getting in between your feet and tripping everyone up. It'd just come to leaving it in a corner the whole evenin', in the long run, and that'd be half a crown extra to pay and all for nothing."

"I don't want to be a knight," said the young man gloomily. "I look the complete ass in armour—always did."

"There ain't so much armour to the costume as all that," said Vera encouragingly.

The young man shook his head.

"Do you fancy Julius Cæsar?" said Miss Dupré. "The last gentleman we let it out to—well, it was a young lady, to be exact—put a stencil pattern round the 'em. Cool, wasn't it? but I must say it's smartened up the costume. See if you can lay 'ands on it, Vera."

"It takes more than a toga to make Cæsar," said Mr. Blakeney, stroking his nose, which was a short one—rather a nice nose, thought Katherine, and going quite attractively with fair hair and a short, clean-cut jaw. You could imagine Mr. Blakeney running and jumping and not getting too much out of breath. It was a pity he was such a nuisance about his clothes. Meditatively he looked about, stretched a hand to a heap of false noses, chose out a Roman beak, and, clapping it on, regarded Miss Dupré mournfully.

"You see what the costume demands," he said. "And I'd rather wear chain-mail than an extra nose."

"It don't suit you, I must say," stated Vera.

Mr. Blakeney quickly removed it and looked with some concern at Katherine, whom he seemed to see for the first time.

"When in doubt, it's much easier to rig up a funny costume than a serious one," said she. "Why don't you go as a fairy or a scarecrow?"

Mr. Blakeney was thrilled at once.

"Oh, I'd love to be a fairy," he said. "Why didn't I think of that before?" And he glanced round the tumbled stock with new hope.

"You'll get no fairy costume for a gentleman here," said Miss Dupré, with a sniff. "And you won't get one anywhere. There's no demand, and I'm glad there isn't."

"I was a scarecrow once at school," said Katherine, wishing he hadn't seized with such avidity on an idea that little Miss Dupré couldn't carry out. "It was quite a good costume."

"I don't see why I shouldn't look the part," said Mr. Blakeney. It was safe for him to say it.

"I've got the old coat I wore up in my room," cried Katherine, suddenly remembering she had wrapped her books in it when she left home. "It's a beauty—really green with age, and with lovely tatters, and a topping patch. Wait—half a sec—find an old hat for him, Vera, one that'll squash right down over his face so that he'll look as if he hadn't got one."

Forgetful of everything but the joy of "dressing up", she flew off, and, in a surprisingly short time, returned with the coat.

"What luck that I brought it! Hold out your arms—you must keep them stiff out, and move as if you were waggling a bit in the wind."

"Oh, *rather*!" said Mr. Blakeney. "I can do that all right."

"This costume is supplied by the Maison Dupré, you know," said Katherine in a low voice, for she saw that Miss Dupré, from her sofa, was looking a little worried, perhaps with the thought that the fee for a scarecrow might be paltry compared with that for the Red Cross Knight or Julius Cæsar, and, such as it was, might be diverted to a mushroom rival.

"Oh yes, of course," said Mr. Blakeney. "How do I look?"

"First-rate. ... A dead crow or two, of course, would add to it. You haven't any birds, Miss Dupré?"

"I'm not a poulterer or a fishmonger, Miss Lovatt," stated Miss Dupré, with dignity.

Katherine glanced for a second at a stuffed owl in a glass case rather too small for it, decided that it was no good, and rolled up the scarecrow outfit with speed and precision.

"Seven and six fee," she said, handing it to him. "And two and six deposit."

He took out a treasury note, and put it on the table, looking at her with a twinkle, as if he knew she was just pretending, but she avoided his eye.

"How do I look?"

"I hope you'll find the costume satisfactory," she said. "Good night."

"Well, it's the first time I've seen a scarecrow go out of my establishment," said Miss Dupré.

Katherine just wondered.

"But 'e seemed pleased. Seven and six! Why, that's the price of Friar Tuck, with wig, and the lady of the time of Charles I. You've got the knack, Miss Lovatt, and I'm very much obliged to you."

"It's fun," said Katherine.

"Of course, if you just cared to assist me a bit, while I'm laid up—I don't say as the salary'd be 'andsome, but we'd go shares. But it mightn't be the kind of work—"

"I'd like it," said Katherine. "Or at least, I'd like to try."

III

It was a big room, painted white, with cloudy dark-blue curtains stencilled in vermilion and gold. The floor was polished. Gaily coloured Chinese lanterns swung in a string from one wall to another. You could pull the window curtains, click on the electric switch, and, standing before a long mirror, see how you would look on the night. Behind the wall curtains were rows and rows of carnival dresses. For ten and six you could be funny—and the Dupré and Lovatt comic costumes were always changing, always showing fresh ideas; for a guinea you could be beautiful. In a cupboard were masks and wigs and various kinds of make-up— quite soon Katherine had discovered that it paid to sell the rouge and powder and lipstick and kohl that the costumes demanded. You could call on the night of the party, if you liked, and Miss Lovatt would make you up as your just-for-the-evening character. Only five shillings—and she did it most excellently.

She knew so well that people are all different, that every face and figure demands special treatment, and she knew that for all individuals there are fancy dresses which are *theirs*, that in these strange or long-ago carnival clothes they may be more truly themselves than in their twentieth-century dress. And she really seemed to *care*—she triumphed when she discovered in her stock what was "right", and she would alter this—and this—and this— or rather, she would hand over the garment to that busy and cheerful little Miss Dupré for alterations. And the things were always so *clean*, and the colours so good. And directly you entered that room with the cloudy curtains and the glowing lanterns you felt the fun of the party. There was a mysteriousness about it and a gaiety; and the heads of the firm seemed to be enjoying themselves, as if they too were already there. No wonder Dupré and Lovatt got on.

"And it was all through that little street," said Katherine suddenly one late afternoon, as she sewed a black cap to go with the harlequin's costume that, in all the brilliancy of its five colours, lay on the stool beside her. "And the funny thing is, Miss Dupré, that that little street is *lost*. I've been back again and looked for it. It was—well, there was something about that street. I wanted to see it again."

"And there's the yaller skirt you wanted, though I'd 've liked you in white myself, as a columbine," said Miss Dupré, shaking the filmy thing, light as a puff of dandelion down. "But I must say what you like generally does look well."

"D'you remember how Jimmy wanted to be a fairy?" said Katherine. "That first night, quite a long time ago?"

"Well, 'e's got on, anyway," said Miss Dupré. "From a scarecrow to 'arlequin. It's an improvement. I wouldn't fancy a scarecrow to dance with, myself."

"Oh," said Katherine. "That depends. … But isn't it strange about that street—that little lost street?"

"I'll lay I could find it," said Miss Dupré. "Certingly I know its appearance. I sat there lookin' 'elplessly about me long enough."

"Perhaps I don't want it found," said Katherine. "Perhaps it's better to leave it as it is, without putting up in it a monument to the good luck it brought."

"You monument off and see to your Columbine slippers," said Miss Dupré, "or you'll keep 'arlequin waiting when 'e comes to escort you to the ball."

The Two Silver Kings

BY EVELYN SMITH

I

L intie, dear, I wish you wouldn't waste so much time gazing out of the window. Have you done your homework?"

The small girl who had been kneeling on a high stool looking out across the housetops lowered one leg and felt for the floor with her foot.

"She hasn't," said Lintie's sister Judith, glancing at a page of blotted sums which lay open near her own neat book.

"I do so hate fractions," murmured Lintie, coming slowly to the table.

"You won't when you can do them. Come and tackle them, dear—you must work hard and try to get on."

"*I'm* getting on," said Laura. "There's nobody else only thirteen in my form. I'm the youngest. And I asked Miss Falconer if I might go in for the prize poem competition. And she said yes."

"I don't know about writing poetry," said Mrs. Day. "I don't think any of you could do that—except Anne, perhaps. But you can do your lessons, and make the most of what it's rather difficult to give you, just now."

The three settled down with deep sighs. Lintie frowned at her sums. The others, remembering the beauty of the outlook from the country house where they had lived before their father died, could not think why she liked staring out of a town window. But the chimney-pot families were so interesting. Nearly every single chimney was fitted with a differently shaped cowl for carrying away the smoke. There was one like a bishop with a mitre; there was one like a pawn from Anne's chess-board, with his head bent a little and his body scooped out. It was dreadful to see him swing round with the wind, smoke pouring out of him as if he were burning to death. If he had squeaked as he whirled about, as his neighbour in the neat helmet did, it would have been quite unbearable, and perhaps the two silver kings would have done something about it. For the silver kings had power, Lintie was sure of it.

They were really splendid chimneys, side by side on their own private stack, tall and glistening. Their silvery tin cowls, cut out at the top like crowns, fitted low down on them; it was unbelievable that, underneath, they should be ordinary affairs of brick and mortar, like the dull folk who just smoked, and did not whirl with the wind. They shone in sun, rain, and starlight; even when the fog came down, Lintie could see them dimly. She never wearied of making up stories about them, of how they had come to rule the roofs, of the good they had done, of the troubles they had had, especially with that Smoky Pawn, and his squeaking neighbour, for ever complaining, and refusing every scheme to oil him that might be set afoot. They were as good as a book, but Lintie found that she could not think of their affairs unless she could see them. That was why she knelt at the window so often, staring out, as if, said Laura, the circus at least were going past.

"*Now* I've done them, horrid old things!" Lintie looked about for a piece of blotting-paper, seized a new white sheet that lay by Laura's pencil-box, and smacked it triumphantly on her book. Then she raised it, and her expression of exultation turned to one of dismay as she saw the untidy black blur which was her exercise.

"Lintie! You little silly! That's not blotting-paper!"

Obviously it was not. Lintie gazed at her sums.

"It's a lovely bit of paper I was saving for my poem," grumbled Laura.

"Well, you're not the only person who's going to write a

They were really splendid chimneys

poem," said Lintie, ripping out the page, mortified. "I'm going to write one myself."

"Ode to a Blot," said Judith.

"Sonnet to a Smudge," suggested Laura.

"Never mind, Lintie," said Mrs. Day. "Just try it."

"I'm going to," said Lintie determinedly.

"*What's* it to be called, Lintie?" coaxed Laura, quite seriously.

"I can't tell you," said Lintie, "it's a secret. But I know."

II

Lintie said nothing more of her scheme. For a little she thought of telling Anne, grave, dreamy, and yet interested in what other people did, a good person in whom to confide; but Anne, when she came home that evening, was worried about her own affairs. Her time at the Art School would soon be over. She had shown promise, and her masters wanted her to devote herself to her work, but she knew that she could not remain dependent while she tried to make good. "If only I could get a start," she said despondently. "Posters, illustration, anything—it would be all right, I know, if I could find someone to begin wanting my stuff and paying for it. But I might have to wait years. No, I'll just have to teach, and I suppose I'll get used to it."

Obviously Anne was not in the mood for the ambitions of other people, and Lintie resolved that her poem should be a secret.

It had been in her mind for so long that it was not difficult to write, and she had posted it and forgotten it when, one afternoon in prep, Sadie Bennett, her lively, inquisitive neighbour, leant across to her desk and asked for her atlas. She passed it over, and then, seeing Sadie's sudden interest and entertainment, realized that the rough copy of her poem lay between the maps of Scotland and England. Quickly she retrieved atlas and poem, but Sadie did not let the matter rest.

"Do you know what Lintie Day has been writing poetry about?" she said, as the girls put on their outdoor things in the cloakroom. "Chimney-pots!"

"Chimney-pots! How romantic! Did you send it in for the comp, Lintie?"

"Do let me look at it!"

"I won't."

"Naughty temper. I say, Laura, did you know that Lintie has written a poem, all by herself, all about chimney-pots?"

Laura did not. However, she rose to the occasion.

"It's more than you could do, anyway," she retorted. "Ready, Lin?"

With a fierce look at her critics, Lintie followed Laura from the cloakroom. She hoped that she had heard the last of her unfortunate poem, but, over home-lessons that evening, Judith opened fire.

"Chimney-pots! How romantic!"

"You might let me see it, Lintie. Imagine, Anne, Lintie has written a poem—and it's about chimney-pots!"

"Why shouldn't it be?" said Anne, from behind the evening paper. "Is it about the ones you look at when you look out of the window, Lintie?"

"The ones like kings with crowns," said Lintie in a low shy voice.

"Show me," said Anne, getting up. "And then show me poem."

"The top window's the best—the one in the nursery—I mean schoolroom."

Anne followed her small sister, and gazed out over the house-tops as if she saw them for the first time.

"*Oh!* Oh, *what* a water-colour I could do of this to-night—just roofs and sky and the chimneys—those queer lovely chimneys!"

She stared and stared as intently as ever Lintie had done. Then she whisked off for her water-colour box and her block and her brushes. Lintie wished she had remembered to ask to read the poem. But she was glad that Anne was so greatly impressed—it seemed as if there must be something in the two silver kings.

III

Anne worked her sketch up into a picture, "The Two Silver Kings", which was hung in the Students' Exhibition, and, to Lintie's delight, won a good deal of praise. She wondered if Sadie and company knew about it, but did not attempt to discover, thinking it wiser not to remind them in any way of what they seemed to have forgotten, her unlucky poem.

Then, one morning near the end of term, Miss Leigh, the headmistress, announced after prayers that she would give out the results of the prize poem competition, and read the best efforts, as she called them. Lintie wished she could become invisible. Sadie turned round and stared at her with a malicious little grin. How terrible—how unendurable it would be if Miss Leigh read

out the worst as well as the best; if she had resolved to give a
booby prize, and the chimney-pots won it, and the whole school
roared with laughter at them. Lintie thought of that roar and
quaked. Should she rush away if it came, or should she just stand
still and pretend she didn't care? She would stand still, and she'd
look at the left leg of the table on the platform, and nowhere
else.

"'Sweet Daphne' deserves special mention in the middle class,
but her poem is a little inclined to gush——"

Lintie pricked up her ears. "Sweet Daphne" was Laura. She
had missed the names of the senior people who had done extra
well.

"There are one or two pretty little poems from the juniors,
but there is one which is far and away the best, recording what
has pleased and interested the writer, saying what she has really
seen and fancied about a thing, not what she thinks is 'poetical'.
This is called 'The Two Silver Kings' and is by 'Top Window'.
Will 'Top Window' please come up and get her prize?"

In her delighted excitement Lintie almost ran up. The girls
laughed at her, but in a friendly way, and everyone clapped hard
as Miss Leigh gave her her prize, a guinea to be spent on books.
Never had she had such a happy day in school.

An odd thing was that Judith and Laura and the Lower Third
seemed to have forgotten how much they had teased her about
the subject of her poem, and congratulated her as if they were
not a bit surprised, but had guessed at this great result all the
time.

"You see what it is to try," said Mrs. Day, when she heard the
joyful news at tea-time. It was almost as if she too had foreseen
the surprising event.

"Isn't it *lovely*?" said Lintie, eating bread-and-butter much too
fast because she was excited. "Isn't it a *glorious* surprise for you,
Mother?"

"Tell Lintie your glorious surprise, Anne," said Mrs. Day.

And Anne told how a publisher who was issuing a series of books on the great towns of Britain had seen "The Two Silver Kings" in the exhibition, and had been so much pleased with it that he had commissioned her to do illustrations in water-colour for these books—work that was well paid and would probably lead to more of the same kind.

Lintie hugged Anne, and went to the window to look out. Tea was in the schoolroom that afternoon, and there was a good view of the kings.

"Come back, Lintie!" cried Judith. "There's a bun that's yours, still."

"Oh, let her have one look," said Anne. "They've done us both such a very good turn. She really must say thank you—thank you to the two silver kings."

Books to Treasure

Old favourites

E M CHANNON:
The Cinderella Girl
A Countess at School
Expelled from St Madern's
A Fifth Form Martyr
The Handsome Hardcastles (print)
Her Second Chance
The Honour of the House (eBook only)

E E COWPER (eBook only):
Camilla's Castle
The Mystery Term
The Holiday School

SARAH DOUDNEY (eBook only):
Monksbury College
When We were Girls Together

EVELYN EVERETT-GREEN (eBook only):
Queen's Manor School

E L HAVERFIELD (eBook only):
The Ghost of Exlea Priory
The Discovery of Kate

sales@bookdragonbooks.co.uk   www.bookdragonbooks.co.uk

RAYMOND JACBERNS (eBook only):
A School Champion
The Record Term

BESSIE MARCHANT (eBook only):
By Honour Bound
To Save Her School!
The Two New Girls

DOROTHEA MOORE (eBook only unless specified):
A Plucky Schoolgirl (Manor School 1)
The Making of Ursula (Manor School 2)

Brenda of Beech House
Fen's First Term
Head of the Lower School
Her Schoolgirl Majesty
A Runaway Princess
Septima Schoolgirl
Séraphine-Di Goes to School
Tam of Tiffany's
Wanted: an English Girl (print & eBook)
The Wrenford Tradition (print & eBook)

WINIFRED NORLING:
The Quins at Quayle's

EVELYN SMITH:
Seven Sisters at Queen Anne's (Queen Anne's 1)
Septima at School (Queen Anne's 2)
Phyllida in Form III (Queen Anne's 3)

eBooks available for download from all Amazon sites

Evelyn Smith (cont)
Val Forrest in the Fifth (Myra Dakin's 1) (eBook only)
Milly in the Fifth (Myra Dakin's 2)

Biddy and Quilla
Binkie of IIIb
The First Fifth Form
The Little Betty Wilkinson
Marie Macleod, Schoolgirl
Nicky of the Lower Fourth
The Small Sixth Form

Ethel Talbot (eBook only unless specified):
The Girls of the Rookery School
The New Girl at the Priory (print & eBook)

Theodora Wilson Wilson (eBook only):
Founders of Wat End School
The St. Berga Swimming Pool

Also available from Books to Treasure:

HELEN BARBER:
The Princess and the Socks

PHILIP S DAVIES:
Destiny's Rebel (Rebel 1)
Destiny's Revenge (Rebel 2)

ADRIANNE FITZPATRICK:
Spirit Wings

WENDY H JONES:
The Dagger's Curse (Fergus & Flora Mysteries 1)

ELEANOR WATKINS:
The Village

A J WEAVER:
Be Quiet, Bird!
Big Cats, Little Cats

Lightning Source UK Ltd.
Milton Keynes UK
UKOW06f1246160717
305407UK00001B/37/P